THE STORYTELLER WITH
NIKE AIRS
and other Barrio Stories

Kleya Forté-Escamilla

aunt lute books
SAN FRANCISCO

First Edition

10 9 8 7 6 5 4 3 2 1

Aunt Lute Books
PO Box 410687
San Francisco, CA 94141

Cover Art: "La Ofrenda" (mural) by Yreina Cervantez
Cover and Text Design: Pamela Wilson Design Studio
Typesetting: JBWiley, Drago Design

Senior Editor: Joan Pinkvoss
Managing Editor: Christine Lymbertos

Production:	Nadia Bratt	Cathy Nestor
	Martha Davis	Loana Valencia
	Jonna K. Eagle	Kathleen Wilkinson
	Vita Iskandar	

Production Support:	Cristina Azócar	Jamie Lee Evans
	Siobhan Brooks	Melissa Levin
	Rebecca deGuzman	Fabienne McPhail
	Michelle Uribe	Jee Yeun Lee

Printed in the U.S.A. on acid-free paper.

Library of Congress Cataloging-in-Publication Data

Forté-Escamilla, Kleya, 1942-
    The storyteller with Nike airs, and other barrio stories / Kleya Forté-Escamilla.
—1st ed.
      p.   cm.
    Contents: Voices overheard at the Ochoa Street reunion—Esperanza y consuelo—Black orchid—Old lady gin and the magic piano—Ribbon of Fire—Storyteller with Nike airs—The pan birote—Adonde vive Dios?—Come rain or come shine—El velatorio de chapa Diaz—Two rock blues—Coming of age—The painter and the vampire.
    ISBN 1-879960-34-6 (alk. paper) : $8.95
    1. Hispanic Americans—Southwestern States—Fiction.   I. Title.
PS3556 . 07485N55   1994
813' .54—dc20   94-29817
                                                CIP

Black Orchid was first published in *Sinister Wisdom* 47 (Summer/Fall 1992): 78-81.
Coming of Age was first published in *Join in Multiethnic Short Stories by Outstanding Writers for Young Adults*, ed. Donald R. Gallo. New York: Bantam Doubleday Dell, 1993.

The Pan Birote was first published in *Saguaro Literary Journal* 7 (1991): 41-47, The University of Arizona; and in *Pieces of the Heart: New Chicano Fiction*, ed. Gary Soto. San Francisco: Chronicle Books, 1993.

The mural, "La Ofrenda," is located on Toluca Street, under the 1st Street Bridge (near the intersection of 2nd and Glendale) in Los Angeles. Yreina Cervantez's youth assistants were Claudia Escobedes, Erick Montenegro, Vladimir Morales and Sonia Ramos.

"La Ofrenda" is a homage to the strength of the Latino people. It brings attention to the hardships of war and immigration and emphasizes women's roles...

This book was funded in part by a grant from the National Endowment for the Arts.

Dedicada a Maria Coatlalopeuh,
Nuestra Señora de Guadalupe
La que me dio la salud y el poder
Para escribir este libro

Y
Con todo corazon para mi abuelita,
La Prieta, la unica madre que tuve

Tambien
Para mi querido hermano, Sonny,
1936-1992
AMOR SIN FIN

ACKNOWLEDGEMENTS

I cannot put into words the gratitude I feel to my editor, Joan Pinkvoss, for helping me bring this book into being; and for her dedication to the uncovering and building of women of color writers. I could not have come this far without her strength and her love; also to the women of Aunt Lute Books, especially Jamie and Chris and the others whom I've never spoken with, but whose struggles and victories reveal themselves in the books they produce. Thank you all.

Gracias tambien to the people who shared the life of the Barrio with me; my beloved grandmother and brothers; and my son, Eden, for his constant love and support.

I wish to thank the Astraea Foundation too, for making it possible for me to write this book.

Comadres,

The Barrio Stories are my memories, the voices I hear in my waking dreams. Voices that are my own voice, but are not my own.

Perhaps I won't accept that they are gone, the place, the world, the people, and so I keep them alive, regardless of the danger to my own soul. Or perhaps, the more I let go of them, the more alive they become, surrounding me, making me a part of the one Life, with them.

I only know the dust of the Barrio still clings to my skin, and I'm glad I could never wash it off.

Love, Kleya

Table of Contents

THE STORYTELLER WITH

NIKE AIRS

and other Barrio Stories

Voices Overheard at the Ochoa Street Reunion

Compadre Alejandro:

"Hey, carnales! Andale, Lupita, kick up those heels. We got to sing and dance, para que se vian los espantos, kick those devils right out of us. We got to drink some copitas and sing. That's the only way to get rid of these condenado blues."

Herlindita a su hermana, Sylvia:

"Ay Sylvia, pero para que te lujes, hermana? Why dress to the teeth? Danny won't be here anyway. He's going out with that rich gringa from El Encanto. He's not gonna look at—what did she call you?—cheap, overmade-up barr-i-o trash. You never should'a let him get fresh. So what if he said he loved you and made promises. Where's the ring, huh? Ahora te dejo aplastada and all you got to show for it is a big stomach, right? Don't cry, it's not the worse thing that could happen, right?"

Viejo Anaya:

"Oye, Vieja, remember how we used to climb in the old car and go pick fruit? Te acuerdas how la Migra used to come at two in the morning and make everybody show their papers and the wetbacks would come out running five minutes before—how did they know? And then they'd come back, making it to the corner, patas heladas, freezing en las mañanitas, waiting for the truck to the fields. Y que uva, que va, grapes from here to Long Beach. And we picked them all. Remember the pie factory in Fresno? The three-day-old pies? And Sundays, eating the pies with our fingers en el parque, like we were on vacation someplace. How fast Sundays were gone, and then we were breaking our backs in the fields again, pero de veras. Remember the mosquitos? We don't even want to remember, no? Then the apricots, peaches, cherries, Oregon, Washington and then Phoenix, New Mexico, Texas...and the old car could barely carry all of us."

Vato, Nazario Rodrigues:

"Remember how messed up Angel was when he came back from the Army? Remember how he said the Tejanos would gang up and beat the shit out of him? And he was the one they'd put in the stockade! Como se moria para irse, y despues le peso. Man, he couldn't wait to get out. It was the Army that killed him—maldito servicio—not because he went off the cliff, but not because something was wrong with the car. His heart blew up, man. Se le apago el corazon."

Tele Bolkan a la Mujer Que Quiso:

"Andale amor, remember how we walked through the canyon that time like walking inside a painting—the paloverde yellow—green, the earth red and ripe with spring? Remember where we stopped, como venia bien jelada l'agua, the stream falling over the rocks? Y nosotros, standing in the water eating papaya, letting the juice run through our fingers like desire...how we couldn't stop eating?"

Vieja Salazar:

"Ahi, hija, nunca se me va olvidar, how I came home from burying el viejo ya no avia nada, everything was gone. Not a stick of furniture was left in the house. Entonces, I put the baby down to sleep—on the floor, porque no avia mas. Que hacia? And then I started to pray. What more could I do?"

Salcido Fermin:

"I don't know how to tell you this, so you'll understand what I'm saying. She was sweet, man, like Carta Blanca in the sun. The day they made us stop seeing each other was the worst day of my life. But jacking off myself was better sometimes, you know what I mean? She was neat, man, I'm telling you."

4

Comadre a Comadre:

"Por que te ries sola, comadre, laughing all by yourself?"

"Bueno, pues, I was remembering one time, maybe I was fifteen or sixteen, and this guy wanted to, well, go with me. I was much too young but he kept coming around anyway. And one day—you know my abuelita, how she used to like to play jokes?—well, she thought she'd play one on her viejo, who was out in the yard, working in the garden. Well, fulano came at about the same time and came around the back to get a drink of water from the faucet. Meanwhile, Abuelita—you know she couldn't see too good anyway—she thought it was her viejo from the back, bending over the faucet drinking water, and she reached down and grabbed his huevos and gave them a good jalada, saying, `Ding-dong, ding-dong.' Well, I didn't know what happened, but we saw fulano go by the window, la cara como lumbre, his face burning red. `What happened to so and so?' I asked. `Pues, I don't know,' my mother said, `but I saw him go by the window in a hurry.' Bueno, no se volvio a parar! We never saw him again!"

Tele Bolkan:

"Mira, amor, so what if we can't be open in front of everybody? Mujer, your lips are as bright and juicy as cherries—they're nuestras gentes, you know, our people! We can't just give that up, can we? Come on, sal conmigo a la noche. I'll take you up to the canyon. We'll walk under the moonlight and I'll braid your hair with it. You'll glow like an angel. We'll stand in the stream and burn, and when we can't stand it anymore, we'll stand under the falls and we'll make each other remember everything."

Sylvia a su hermana, Herlindita:

"You don't have to worry about me. I hate Danny now. There was a time, God, I loved him so much. I can hardly remember it. And then, later, he'd come over y lo aborreci para siempre, I couldn't stand to even *look* at him. Pobre mi hito, turning around inside of me. Think he'll know I hated his father? Nah, he'll never know from me how it was at the end. Nunca va saber. Don't worry, I won't do nothing bad—having my son is the only thing I care about now."

Salcido Fermin:

"Yeah, I know, I shouldn't have run out on her...but shit, man, they broke us up and I wasn't ready to get married. I would've had to give up college, man; her old man would've made us live with them and everything. Can you just see me, jalando newspapers every day at 5:00 in the morning. And coming home to that cara podrida of her mother—shit, she would've even expected me to stay home nights. Hell, I know I can't ever show my face in L.A. again, but Arizona's a better school, anyway, and you know the vatas here, man, they're ready for me..."

Vieja Salazar:

"Bueno, sure, el viejo me dejo sin un centavo, not one penny when he died. But at least he never hit me. He wasn't like those men that get drunk every payday and then come home and kick their wives around. No, era muy bueno conmigo, he treated me good. On paydays, when he was working steady, he always came home with something for me—a purse or a hat—every Saturday.

Todavia tengo en la petaquia los regalos que me traia. They're still in the trunk. I never even got a chance to use them all before he died."

Vato Nazario Rodrigues:
"Si, lo vi esa noche. We had a few drinks, but Angel wasn't even weaving when he left. I donno what happened—he said he was going home, not up the mountain. I should'a gone with him, but he said he was gonna go and sleep it off. Que se queria dormir para siempre. No kidding, man, that's what he said. Do you think he knew something was gonna happen? Maybe that's how it happens to everybody on the last day...do you know what he said the only good thing about the Army was? La comida, man! Steak every day, as much as he could eat. He was this skinny little weasel when he went away, y lo viste? He looked good lying down in his traje. Man, he filled out, pero guapo. The uniform fit him like a glove."

Viejo Anaya:
"Remember ese hombre I told you went crazy in the peach orchard? He started eating the peaches he was picking, up there on the ladder. We were breaking our backs, hauling those heavy buckets full of peaches down and scratching at the peach fuzz down our necks, pero, que va, the peach pits and half-eaten peaches started raining on our heads—creiamos que se avia rajado el cielo. Good thing the foreman wasn't around, pero, que va, finally he started throwing up all over, big chunks of green peaches, and then he slipped on his own basca, dancing around up there

on the ladder. He fell off. Pero, que va, pobre perro, callo como una piedra. He hit the ground like a stone."

Comadre a Comadre:

"Bueno, todito se acaba, no? Everything ends. Pobrecita Abuelita, tan mala que se veia al ultimo, she was so sick we could hardly hold her down. Y, crying for her viejo, que ya, años tenia de muerto, and he'd been dead for so long. I know, para que la tristeza, no? What good does it do to get sad, ya los vivos tenemos que vivir. The living have to get on with living, and she would have loved this party. She loved fiestas. She loved to laugh. Se tomaba una copita, y ya, se ponia a cantar, y que bonita voz tenia, one drink and she'd start singing. Anyway, the street's still the same, no? Mira, the young people are still coming back—they have the Barrio in their blood. Es la Raza. Nothing can keep them away from the neighborhood. You can't take it away from them. I mean, why should they have to go anywhere else?"

Compadre Alejandro:

"Ya, dance with me one more time, Lupita. Maybe the next time I won't be here. Or quizas, you'll have a husband, and then that's it. Come on, I'm old, but I can still have a good time. Dance with me, beautiful Lupita, so I can remember what it is to be young again. Only dance with me, y quien dira que no fui feliz? No one can say I was never happy."

Esperanza y Consuelo

There was a very old woman named Esperanza and her young granddaughter, Consuelo. They lived in a one-room makeshift house at the edge of the desert. Behind them stretched miles of paper shacks like theirs and bare patches of rock-filled dirt where not even a mesquite could grow. Before them lay the endless body of the open desert.

Esperanza and Consuelo survived by making calditos out of whatever they could find. Each day, while her abuelita walked in the desert looking for wild greens, Consuelo walked the streets. She searched for stray vegetables or damaged cans among the boxes thrown away behind las tienditas de los chinos. These last she never let her abuelita see because the old woman feared anything that came from a can.

Sometimes Consuelo washed her dress and went to the big supermercado where los americanos came in their grand cars to shop. She asked them for work cleaning their houses or ironing shirts. But they were afraid of her few words of English, and although her young woman's body was hidden by the shapeless rag she wore, her face was that of an angel. Maybe she would cause trouble among the men of the house. No, better not to let her in. And, too, they were afraid she was just a front to find out what they had in their houses, and later others would come back to steal from them. So there was seldom anything for Consuelo to do. One or two men, who looked of an age to have a daughter like her, were ashamed before her poverty and gave her the change from their pockets. Most people pushed past her, pretending not to see or hear, easily ignoring her quiet voice, her slight figure and expressionless face. It didn't matter one way or the other to Consuelo. She already knew what the world was.

One night Esperanza had a dream. She dreamed she was walking in a strange but familiar place, and it began to sprinkle. She found a big mesquite and crawled under it. She held her knees and wondered where Consuelo was, why she did not see her house. El agua se quedo lloviznando; it wasn't real rain, just a steady drizzle, not enough to water anything, just enough to wet the face of the earth. So Esperanza covered her head with her rebozo and continued walking. However, she didn't know which direction to take or even where she was going. She looked around, and everywhere she looked, vio puro oro, there was gold.

That morning when Consuelo awakened her, saying, "Dime tus sueños, Abuelita. What did you dream last night?" the old woman said, "Pues, vi un tesoro aqui, I know there's a treasure of gold someplace around here." She made Consuelo go outside the house with her and she pointed here and there, and the girl dug a hole in each place. But they found nothing.

"Estoy segura que vi un tesoro, I know that's what I saw," Esperanza would say. "It has to be here." Each morning they searched again, Esperanza hanging onto Consuelo's arm as they walked, one slow step at a time. Esperanza kept herself standing upright by leaning on a stick while Consuelo dug with the shovel. One day they tried at the foot of a big mesquite. Another day they went a few feet past the ravine at the back of the house and dug there. After each failure to find something, Esperanza grew more silent. It was her last chance to give something to the girl she thought of as her own daughter. The days went by and she would not give up hope, but only God knew why He did not give them the treasure.

Finally one day, Esperanza went to bed and did not get up again. Each night she went a little farther away, walking a little deeper into the desert, and the desert began to close around her. Sometimes, on returning, she saw the golden light cast by a tesoro of gold. And after that she would sleep the best sleep of all, until she felt Consuelo touching her face, her hair, sitting close to her, touching her all over to see if she still lived. Then Esperanza would tell Consuelo about the gold again, smacking her lips around the words, moving her tongue around in her mouth, as though it was this that fed her.

One morning, Esperanza pushed the spoon away when Consuelo tried to feed her. Afterward, Consuelo went to the place past the ravine where she had already dug a hole and started to dig it deeper. Each day she dug the hole bigger and deeper, a little at a time, because she did not have much strength either.

Like clouds rising into the sky during the desert monsoon season, como nuves subiendo a el cielo, so Esperanza and La Muerte got closer together, and then she saw the tesoro of gold again. The light was so bright. She had forgotten about it and here it was, like the sun coming up. Maybe that was what it was. She heard a rooster crowing and it was like the sound of her own voice coming from her breast. All at once she came all the way out of herself, through her heart. She stood in the middle of the desert, surrounded by saguaros with thorns of light and blooming flowers of gold. And she knew she never had to go back again.

After Esperanza was covered up in the grave Consuelo had dug for her at the mouth of the desert, Consuelo began to clean everything. She took Esperanza's bed apart. The mattress came away in pieces, rotten ancient tendido as old as its owner. Consuelo carried the pieces outside and piled them next to the ravine. Then she dragged the iron bed to a place beside the mattress. She swept the floor of the house twice and cleaned the wooden boards with water. As she sat back on her haunches to rest, she saw a crack where two boards fit together and without paying too much attention, tried to move the boards apart. A section, encrusted with dirt, came away neatly in her hands. And there, more than a foot below the floorboards, stood a small cochito, covered with dirt and spider webs.

Consuelo had to lift it out with both hands, the pig was so heavy. The ceramic cochito had a curly tail and its body was painted all over with big red and blue flowers. Consuelo brushed the pig off and turned it over. Holding it in the air, she jiggled it back and forth and a big toston de oro fell out. It vibrated from side to side on the wooden floor and then lay still, a gleaming spot of gold. When Consuelo saw what it was, she began to cry. She wiped her eyes with her hands and rocked and wailed as she had not done the morning her abuelita died. "Ay, Abuelita, aqui esta tu tesoro! Aqui esta tu tesoro de oro, your treasure! Here it is!" she cried over and over again, and she lay on her side beside the hole in the floor, looking at the gold coin that lay before her.

That night Esperanza came to Consuelo, saying, "Hija, este es el tesoro de mi vida. This treasure is my life." And Consuelo asked, "Que quieres que hage con el? Tell me what to do, Abuelita." But there was no answer. Consuelo went and dug a small hole at the foot of Esperanza's grave and buried the cochito there. But the next night Esperanza was back again, and Consuelo could not sleep because the old woman kept whispering, "Es el tesoro de mi vida. This treasure is my life."

One day, Consuelo couldn't stand it anymore. She got up at dawn and dug up the cochito. She carried it with her into the desert. After a while it got so heavy she tied it up in her apron and dragged it behind her by the apron strings. Something pushed at her back and made her walk toward the eastern mountain, from whose face the morning sun always rose. The mountain changed from blue to brown as she reached the foothills and started to climb.

The mountain was very high and the way was treacherous with sharp rocks and deep crevices. Consuelo was so tired she could hardly keep going and when she came to a small level place just big enough she sat down for a moment to rest. She did not know why but she knew she had to reach the top of the mountain before night came. The sun had already lost its brilliance and was beginning to sink down toward the desert.

Consuelo realized there was someone else there on the rocks, a big man in uniform. He scrambled toward her, knocking down some boulders that fell and cracked as they pounded down the mountain. He smiled, showing rotten teeth, and said, "Give me the cochito and I will carry it for you. It is much too heavy for a pretty girl like you." At first Consuelo was tempted. She thought, Why am I carrying this heavy thing to the top of the mountain anyway? But she thought of Abuelita and the strange words she spoke every night. She took another look at the man. Spit was dribbling out of one corner of his mouth. She said, "Gracias, but I don't need any help." The man was barely holding onto a rock with one hand but with the other he tried to grab the cochito. It glowed as red as the wood stove. Snatching his hand back, he squealed and snarled at Consuelo. He reminded her of the rat in the house that was always begging for scraps at her feet and she pitied him. She took a few coins out of the cochito and gave them to him. He slobbered over them and scratched his way around the rocks and out of sight.

It seemed as if she had only gone a few steps when another person appeared, blocking her path. This man had a big mustache like the revolutionaries in Zapata's army. He said, "It is not right for one person to have so much money. Give me the cochito and I will spread the coins among all the people." This sounded very good to Consuelo. After all, she had never had anything in the first place. But she heard Abuelita's voice in her ear, and she told the man, "This cochito does not belong to me. I can't give it to you." At this, the man pulled a big pistola from his belt and pointed it at her. "Give me the cochito," he said, "or I'll kill you because you're nothing but a spoiled rich girl." She did not try to stop him from reaching for the cochito. But he, too, felt the searing heat. He screamed with pain. The pistola fell from his hand and fired, the bullet striking him between his narrow and angry eyes. Consuelo held the cochito to her breast in fear. She shook some coins out over his body and set out once more on the trail to the top of the mountain.

The cochito wasn't so heavy now, and there didn't seem to be as many pointed rocks in her way. She could already see the large boulders above her where the trail would level out on top of the mountain. As she was taking the last few steps, another man jumped in front of her. His great white wings startled her but she was quickly calmed, for this man had a beautiful gentle face and large liquid eyes that seemed to be filled with tears. He stretched out his hands, saying, "Give me the cochito. The gold will only taint your soul, while I, your brother nearest to God, know how to use it: for the good of the world and to save souls." Consuelo thought of her abuelita's words again, *This treasure is my life*, and thought, surely Abuelita would want this kind, compassionate and God-inspired man to help others.

"Will you give the gold in Abuelita's name, then?" she asked.

"Of course, of course, in the name of Abuelita and of God," he said, reaching out his hands to accept the cochito from Consuelo. But when his fingers touched the cochito he screamed in pain, and the wings on his back smelled like burned feathers. "Hija de el demonio!" he screeched, making signs in the air in front of Consuelo. Consuelo walked a little way, leaving a pile of coins on the path behind her. The man with the wings was licking his fingers and crawling toward the gold as Consuelo left.

A little while later, the trail dipped down and delivered Consuelo to a clearing on the top of the mountain. Large, billowing white clouds passed overhead; the air smelled like water and growing things. She drank from a small stream nearby. The ground was covered with lush green quelites. Several tall saguaros with long arms stood in a circle, guarding the clearing. Feeling exhausted, Consuelo sat down. Her bones loose in her body, she pulled the now empty cochito to her side and lay down on the soft desert earth. The shadows lengthened into darkness, and the stars came out shining and laughing all over the black midnight sky. A coyote appeared at the opening to the clearing and padded softly around Consuelo. He gingerly walked up to her as she lay, head in her arms. He sniffed at her feet and sniffed at the cochito. He whined slightly, then jumped away with a short bark. He melted into the darkness of the mountain.

Esperanza's voice came out of the night wind, "Adios, mi tesoro. Adios mi casita. Adios a mi vida. Goodbye."

"Adios a tu vida," echoed Consuelo, never moving her head. Esperanza's spirit lingered over her, but the girl didn't see. The morning sun, rising above the mountain, illuminated the desert and the ravine where Consuelo lay beside Esperanza's grave. She woke in the bright rays of light and seeing where she was, leaped up, frightened, heart pounding. But there was no threat in the sweet sounds of birds and the beauty of the fresh clean morning. Looking down, she saw the cochito had broken, and a pile of gold coins lay spilled at her feet. A flash of light went from the gold into the sun. The brightness that was Esperanza went back into the earth. The desert quivered. The air sang with the old woman's voice, "Hija, ya tengo tu consolacion, you have consoled me."

And Consuelo answered, "Ya tienes tu libertad, Abuelita, y yo, la esperanza de vivir!" Consuelo sang the words once more at Esperanza's grave. "You are free at last, Grandmother, and I have hope of the future!" Then she gathered the gold coins into a bundle and walked away.

Black Orchid

She went down there again the next day after school. A side street not many people passed by. The VFW was across the street but it could have been ten thousand miles away. The bar had no windows at all, a brick wall with a solid door in the middle. The small sign over the door was faded, impossible to read.

Chula inched along the wall, looked both ways, saw no one. So she leaned against the wall right at the edge of the alley, ready to run back. She was a young woman, with a soft, innocent, well-formed face, saddle shoes, a narrow blue skirt and grey sweater, dark intense eyes. She held her schoolbooks locked against her chest. It was mid-afternoon. She waited until the very last minute, until she had to run home to keep from being late.

The next day she came again. It was not a good time for people to be coming to a bar but it was the only time she had and maybe...but no one came.

Chula waited, nervous, practicing to herself what she would say. Maybe she wouldn't have to say anything. Maybe all she had to do was see her and the woman who dressed like a man would understand everything. But another day went by and she didn't come.

Then it was Saturday and Chula came downtown with her Tia to buy some tela for her Home Ec class, but Tia had forgotten her purse. In a rush to get to Tia's house because the store was near closing, they cut through the alley to avoid traffic and get more quickly to the south side of town. Just as they reached the end of the alley and were about to jaywalk across the street, an Impala came around the corner and roared to a stop. The woman Chula had been waiting for all those days got out right in front of them.

Chula saw all of her in one frozen instant: black eyes and molded lips, wild hair brushing her tan cheek, breasts taut beneath a blue western shirt, Levi's ironed and creased, a silver chain hanging from the pocket. Y esas movidas, and that incredible energy. Chula just hung there and Tia tried to pull Chula one way while she stumbled another. The woman who dressed like a man steadied her and stood her on the curb again, saying, "Watch out," in a throaty laughing voice. The air around them was drenched with the hot smells of skin and cologne and Chula's feelings—paralyzed and burning. She stared into the woman's face with lips trembling, and then her Tia jerked her away and across the street as though a rabid dog were at their heels.

Chula started to turn around, catching a glimpse of the woman standing next to the Impala, watching her. But her Tia hissed, "Ponte cara en frente! Don't look over there!"

"Why not?" said Chula.

"Te agarra una de esas, y ningun hombre te quiere de mujer. If one of those women touches you, no man will want you. Do you understand?" Who cares? thought Chula. But she made an effort to keep her face straight and her Tia didn't notice, still talking with disgust and venom in her voice. "Una muchacha como ti son las que quieren. Te siguen y te agarran. They run after young girls like you and ruin you. Never go near that place." She kept her hand firmly on Chula's arm, pulling her along.

The next Saturday Chula got permission to go to the library with her cousins, Amalia and Tootsie, and then she told the girls she had to go buy something in a flash. Already flirting with some cute boys, they hardly noticed her leaving. Chula ran all the way from the library to the back of the building and then up the alley. It was almost time.

Panting, Chula peered around the corner, but there was no Impala. The late afternoon sun was hot and blistery on the pavement. She had waited as long as she dared when she saw the black car coming down the street. Before the woman who dressed like a man could get out, Chula opened the passenger door and jumped in. The woman, startled, stared at Chula.

"Will you take me someplace?" asked Chula. Disbelief, amusement, concern—all struggled in the woman's face. She reached across Chula's breast, pushing her back gently against the seat, and made sure the door was closed. As she double-clutched at the corner, she said, "Where do you want to go?"

"I don't know," said Chula. Her throat got tighter and tighter. She swallowed. "I mean, I just want to be with you."

The woman didn't say anything but drove down a side street skirting the Barrio and along the edge of the South Side. When they came to a piece of desert, she pulled away from the road and stopped the car. She left the engine running.

"You're the one who's been hanging around."

Chula, afraid of the anger in the woman's voice, said, "I've been waiting for you."

"How old are you?" The woman reached out as if to touch her, then pulled her hand back. "Do you know what they'd do to me if they found us together?" Chula heard her fear now. "They'd cut off my hands," the woman said.

"Take me someplace," Chula pleaded.

"Take you where? For what? You have to wait until you're eighteen."

"When I'm eighteen maybe I won't want this anymore."

The woman's voice was soft. "When you're eighteen maybe you won't want this anymore," she agreed.

"Please. I'll never bother you again..."

The woman dropped the car keys she had pulled out of the ignition, found them, and put them back. Her face was pale. "Come on, kid, you'll get me into trouble."

"There's no one I can talk to. There's nobody I can tell about this," Chula said.

The woman drove out on Saguaro Road. She drove all the way with both hands on the steering wheel. They got off the road at a small ranchito. They passed the big house, vacant, windows broken. Further back, behind a stand of tamarack trees, was a little casita with a pink door. Someone had painted a beautiful black orchid on it.

They both got out. The woman leaned against the car. Chula walked around looking at the mountains turning purple, at the dancing tamarack sweet with the voices of birds. It was quiet, she could hear the bees buzzing.

The woman watched her, silent, tense, knowing she'd come back.

She did. With a cry, Chula pressed herself against the woman's body. The woman didn't move, turned her head aside. Chula forced her face against the other's face, put her hands around the hot skin of her neck. The woman's breath quickened but still she didn't lift her arms, only her breast heaved up and down under Chula's breast.

Chula's need was like a pain filling her body but not telling her what to do, how to move. The sensations started in her legs where they pressed against the woman's legs. Small sharp bursts of electricity—the sensations came and went, over and over again, and stronger. She trembled against the older woman's body. Until at last the woman's hands encircled her ass and pressed— that was all—pressed her tighter and held her that way, without moving. The burning turned liquid, flowing into Chula's thighs, bursting between her legs. The woman's own breath came out in a moan of pleasure and despair. But she never moved her body. They stayed like that until Chula stepped back—of her own will.

It was two years later, the day after Chula's eighteenth birthday—the day when Chula had said she'd look for her. It was a Saturday, and that evening she went down to the VFW. She stood in the shadow of the doorway and waited a long time before she saw the black Impala come rumbling to a stop. It had new skirts and whitewall tires. A pink streamer was flying from the antenna.

Chula ducked behind the door and saw the strangely beautiful woman: molded lips, shaggy black hair, strong lean body in a blue denim shirt, sleeves rolled up, new Levi's with a long silver chain hanging from the watch pocket. Chula saw the woman reach for something behind the visor, lock the car doors and step into the bar.

Chula came out of her hiding place and went slowly back the way she'd come. She didn't see the woman come out and follow Chula with her eyes for several long breath-held beats of the heart. Then the woman carefully placed the orchid she was holding in her hand on the fender of the Impala, turned and went back inside.

Chula stopped and stared at the traffic for a while, then crossed the street. A few minutes later, legs shaking, she came back. Slowly approaching the Impala she saw the black orchid, and picked it up with trembling fingers. Chula opened the door of the bar.

Old Lady Gin
And The Magic Piano

"L et's play house," Lea suggested. She was starving for something to eat.

"Okay," said Sylvia and Chuvi, getting all excited. Lea always got the other kids interested in doing things; her enthusiasm was overwhelming and catching. The two sisters got the blankets and chairs, and Lea organized it all into a roof and walls. It was kind of dark but cozy inside, and private.

"Okay, now," said Lea, "if we're going to have a house, we have to have something to eat in it." So Sylvia and Chuvi got the graham crackers and peanut butter and three spoons, and Lea helped them make cracker sandwiches, making sure there were some extra ones. Then they got under the blankets in their playhouse. A minute later, Lea said it was time to eat. Lea kept everyone in the playhouse where no one could see them, especially Mrs. Diaz. Lea tried to be fair, but she was so hungry. She ate faster than Sylvia and Chuvi but with such enthusiasm it was okay with them. When she spooned out the last hunk of peanut butter, and there wasn't that much in the jar anyway, Lea saw Sylvia looking at her kind of funny.

After there was nothing left to eat, Lea played for a little while and then said she had to go. She was walking away from the house when she heard Mrs. Diaz through the open door, talking to her daughters. Lea heard the word "peanut butter." So she ran the rest of the way down the alley.

It was already afternoon. Lea knew the Campfire Girls meeting was at the park, en la Veinte-Dos. This was the day everyone had to pay their dues, but it was a picnic party and Lea had to go. She hadn't even bothered to ask Nana for the fifty cents so she could belong to the club; she knew there wasn't any money—not for dues, not for a Campfire Girls uniform, not for anything. And certainly not so much as fifty cents! Lea didn't tell Nana she was going to the park, she just went. As she passed las casitas del sud, Lea saw the mountains rising behind them. At that moment, her stomach growled loudly and she felt such hunger, such a yearning for something that seemed to be behind the mountains somehow. And all Lea knew was that if only she could go to that place behind the mountains, she would finally not be hungry anymore. Her stomach growled again and she walked faster to get to the picnic.

A long table had been made out of several picnic tables placed end to end and there were tablecloths covering the length of it. A poster with the Campfire Girls insignia was at the head of the table and little Campfire Girls napkins were at each paper plate. Lea pretended she didn't have a care in the world, playing and laughing with the other girls, some of whom already had Campfire Girls uniforms: blue skirts with matching blue hats and sashes that went over the shoulder and across the chest with Campfire Girls pins on them. But all the while Lea was glancing toward the table and the food, waiting for someone else to start looking at the food, so she could get closer to it. Every time Lea saw the Campfire Girl Director looking at her, she laughed bigger and played harder, so she would look like everybody else, not like someone who didn't have her dues money and shouldn't be at the picnic. Finally two other girls thought of eating, and Lea followed them toward the table to look at the potato chips and hotdogs and relish. And then one of the girls discovered the maraschino cherries. Lea had never seen or tasted anything like them before. The big bottle was in the place of honor in the center of the table, round red cherries clearly visible, surrounded by red syrup. Lea watched while the girls opened the jar and each pulled a cherry out of the narrow-necked bottle with her fingers. Then Lea played at being naughty too. While the other girls were giggling with their daring and looking around for the Director, Lea quickly got out two more cherries, cracking their delicious firm roundness against her back teeth, slurping with her tongue at the juice that threatened to squirt from her mouth.

Then everybody began coming in from the playground and gathering around the table. Lea took the chance to drift away before they sat down to eat and would be asked for the fifty cents. Lea was sad and lonely walking away. She would never see that bunch of rich americanitas again. She wished she could belong to something too, like everybody else. But the Campfire Girls uniforms, the new shoes, and most of all the way those girls never seemed to be hungry like her, made her realize that she could never be like them. There was no point crying about it; that's all there was to it.

By the time Lea walked back from la Veinte-Dos to her own Barrio, she had almost forgotten about the Campfire Girls. But she felt her heart hurting and she felt guilty about eating the maraschino cherries knowing she couldn't pay her dues. Those feelings extended behind her like a long snake trailing after her corazon and taking small bites out of it. When Lea got to Gin's store, around the block from her house, her corazon was the size of a frijol, and she was feeling pretty empty.

It was near suppertime. The smells of tortillas and green chili salsa came from the kitchens she passed, teasing and burning her nostrils. Her stomach told her she would die if she didn't find something to eat right away. Nana was probably still sleeping away the heat of the day and wouldn't be cooking anything yet. Lea didn't have a penny to buy something, but she hung out at the corner in front of Gin's store, holding onto a light pole and going around it in circles.

Suddenly she saw a little old Chinese lady standing there watching her. Lea had known Gin's store since she could remember, and the Gins had already seen more than one generation of chicanitos and chicanitas grow up on their Bazooka bubblegum and RC Colas. Lea liked the saladitos best, Chinese plums encrusted with salt that burned the inside of her cheeks and lasted longer in her mouth than any candy. But she'd never seen this old Chinese lady before. She was short and skinny, even smaller than Lea. Her shirt was long—down to her ankles—and she had on black slippers beautifully embroidered with red snakes that had wings. She wore an apron that made her look not too different from Lea's Nana and other nanas she knew. But when the old lady talked, saying she was Grandma, Old Lady Gin, the words came out sounding like Spanish spoken in Chinese. Still, Lea knew exactly what she was saying. When she spoke, Old Lady Gin's eyebrows went up and down over black eyes that were very bright, like burning specks of coal behind her round eyeglasses. The snakes on her black slippers danced around as she moved her toes.

"You play the piano?" she demanded.

"Well, yeah, I can play," said Lea.

"How good you play?" Old Lady Gin demanded again. "How many years you take lessons?"

"I donno, maybe a year." Lea thought back over the few lessons she'd had with old Señora Tellez, who complained every week that she was too old to teach anymore. Her house was always too dark too. Nana had taken Lea there on Sundays after misa, and then paid Señora Tellez with nopalitos y chile or a half dozen big flour tortillas or a saucepan of posole. Lea didn't even remember what the old woman had taught her anymore. All she could remember was how dark it was, how she could barely see the notes when she went there to practice, how Señora Tellez walked funny and never went outside.

"Oh, maybe you don't play so good," asked Old Lady Gin.

"You got the music, I can play it," said Lea stoutly.

"You play and I give you a candy bar." Old Lady Gin's eyes were twinkling. Lea couldn't believe it; she had never known the Gins to give away as much as a gumball, and something in her chest heaved up and opened a wide mouth for the candy.

"What am I gonna play on?" she asked.

"I gotta piano, a nice piano," declared Old Lady Gin.

Lea was surprised again; she never imagined the Gins could have anything like a piano in that tiny little house behind the grocery store, or that Chinese people even knew what pianos were.

"You play, I give you candy bar," Old Lady Gin said again.

"Okay, if you want me to, I'll play," said Lea. Old Lady Gin beckoned to her, and Lea followed her through a little gate, down a brick path and over a cement curb into the house. Inside it was dark, but Old Lady Gin opened a curtain and Lea saw the piano. It was smaller than the one she had played at school, and different, flat and round, not tall and blocky like the one at school and like Señora Tellez's. She sat down on the bench slowly, wondering where the strings were and the little hammers that hit the strings and made notes. She had to know if it was real first.

"Can I open it?" she asked Old Lady Gin.

"Here, I show you." She opened the big round lid and stood it on a little stick for Lea, who looked inside at the wires and hammers, all lying down. She started to put the lid down, but Old Lady Gin stopped her.

"No, when you play, it stay open," she said, motioning Lea to begin. Lea put both hands on the keyboard and went down the scale, and then up again, and then let her hands fall together in full octaves. The rich full sounds the piano made filled her stomach and chest and head; her hands and her foot on the sustain pedal felt the way el gato must feel when she petted him the length of his back and he stretched against her and asked for more. So her body asked for more, and she played the music she had learned at school. It was a piece that made her hands cross over each other and had long holding notes, and now she heard it as if for the first time; the long holding notes reverberated on this piano like deep delicious currents under the moving treble voice. She played it twice, to experience the feel of it.

When she looked up, Old Lady Gin had placed a book of music in front of her, and she started playing what she saw. The piano danced and sang beneath her fingers: pieces with names in some other language or with numbers for titles, words she couldn't read, concertos, voices for piano, sounds she had never heard or thought of, notes that flowed together in unexpected ways, simple and clear, dramatic and surprising, the beautiful and ugly mixing up together to make stories, streams of running water and tongues of fire. When Lea finally stopped playing, her fingers aching, the wonderful sounds the piano made for her went on filling her head, like echoes she would keep hearing forever.

It was already getting dark outside. The palm trees on South Sixth were black against the red sky. The mountains seemed to be standing very close as Lea hurried home. She heard notes in the breeze lifting her hair, in the rocks that gave way beneath her feet. Music, other music she hadn't even played, entered her head like silent ghosts, emerging full-voiced to her ears. She felt like she had run all the way from la Veinte-Dos to Nana's house, sweating, legs trembling, heart pumping, body cold and hot at the same time.

"Adonde estavas?" questioned Nana when she came in. Nana was just taking the posole from the stove. "Ya estava con cuidado, I was worried."

"I'm sorry, Nana, I was at Gin's—Old Lady Gin wanted me to play the piano for her."

"Umph, y que te dio?" said Nana.

"She was going to give me a candy bar, but I forgot about it," said Lea, but then she felt the pockets of her sweater and she heard the crackling of candy bar wrappers. There was a Milky Way in one pocket and a Mounds in the other.

"Here, Nana," she said, giving Nana the Mounds bar because Nana loved coconut.

"Bueno," said Nana, "but don't be hanging around there. Didn't I tell you about what happened to Orozco? Remember how he was going to eat a plate of menudo the chinos made, and there was a little finger sitting there? A whole little finger, because that's how the chinos are. They have a trap door in their house, and you fall down there and nobody will see you again. Entonces, te hacen menudo, you'll end up in the menudo pot!"

"Come on, Nana, there wasn't any trap door at Old Lady Gin's house."

"Y que tenia? So what things did she have inside?" asked Nana, curious in spite of herself.

"Nothing, just this really strange piano that was flat like a pancake, and you opened its hat to play so the sound would come out."

"Ay, cosas de chino, Chinamen's habits," said Nana, crossing herself.

"I don't think so," said Lea, remembering. "It had an American name on it, C-L-A-R-K."

"Bueno, pero no andes pidiendo dulces, don't be asking for handouts over there."

"I didn't! God, she gave it to me!"

"Bueno, pues ya," said Nana. She put the Mounds carefully into the can where she kept the tortillas and put the lid on again.

"Can I eat the Milky Way?" asked Lea.

"Tu cena primero, eat your food first," Nana ordered.

"But I'm not even hungry now," Lea said truthfully. It seemed like she had been starving for years, and all of a sudden, she wasn't.

For many weeks afterward, whenever Lea thought about it, she walked past Gins' in the late afternoon, but she never saw Old Lady Gin outside again. The gate was always locked and the door to the little house always closed and the windows covered up. Summer ended and school began again. There was a new music teacher for the fifth graders, and Lea played her some of the music she remembered from Old Lady Gin's. It didn't sound the same on the school piano, but it still must have been okay, because the teacher sent a note home to Nana. After that, Lea got to play the piano after school for two hours every week, and the music teacher stayed with her and showed her things.

One Saturday, toward the end of the school year, Nana sent Lea to Gin's for some soda crackers for the soup because they were out of tortillas and there wasn't any flour left. Lea got the crackers and was coming out of the store when she saw Herman Gin watering the patch of grass in front of the little house. He was older than her but they went to the same school.

On impulse she said, "Hey, where's your grandma? I haven't seen her for a long time." Herman looked at her with a disgusted look on his face.

"What grandma? There's no grandma here," he said, spraying the hose up and down the yard.

"You know, Old Lady Gin. If she's gone, when is she coming back?"

"Whadayou want her for?" asked Herman.

"I don't know. I just thought she might want me to play the piano for her again or something."

Herman laughed. "You crazy Mexican," he said.

"You're the one that's crazy," said Lea. "Come on, ask her for me."

"There's no piano here and no grandma," said Herman. He put the hose down carefully to water the margaritas and stood by the fence, looking at her.

"Ask her if I can play the piano for her," insisted Lea. "I have some new stuff to show her."

"You can't show her," said Herman, finally. "She's dead."

Lea was struck with sorrow. "Well, when did she die?"

"A long time ago. In China. Before you were born."

Lea went home and told Nana what Herman Gin had said.

"Ya ves?" said Nana. "Es lo que sacas por andando metiendote en casas de los chinos. Now their ghosts are following you."

"He was probably lying," said Lea. "I bet they put *her* into the menudo pot and they don't want us to know." That night Lea dreamed about the C-L-A-R-K piano, and she played again the music she had played that summer afternoon. When she was finished, she woke up. Her head was still filled with the lush melodious sounds of the flat round piano, the music she had played for the teacher at school. She got up, went into the kitchen and turned on the light bulb. She got the tortilla can down from the shelf, opened it and looked inside. In the bottom was a crumpled Peter Paul wrapper, with a small piece of hardened candy still left in it that Nana had forgotten. Funny how hungry I was that day, Lea thought. It was the hungriest I've ever been in my life.

"Yeah, they probably just put her in the menudo pot," she said out loud, and went back to bed.

Ribbon Of Fire

Ruben Camayo saw the Chevy pass the garage in front of the highway like a yellow smear. Christ, she didn't even bother to downshift, he thought, wiping his hands with a greasy rag. While I'm stuck here con este chingado Ford. He looked over at the differential lying on the floor like a pregnant lizard. He grimaced, remembering the choking, sliding, clanking noise when the rear end fell out as she was backing down the driveway. That's how Fords are: always falling apart without any warning. He cursed himself again for falling for the hundred coats of metallic cherry red paint and the smooth compact lines of the skirted '47 coupe, menso yo!

The Chevy looked like a ragged beggar next to the Ford, he thought. But there Alejandra was, burning up the road in that sweet little car with its dual carburetors—that he had installed— and the shiny dual exhaust that emitted not a speck of smoke. Camayo spit and turned his attention back to the pile of metal on the floor.

Coming up on the intersection at Cooney Road, Alejandra braked from long habit. Cooney was just a white ribbon of sand coming in from the west and disappearing in the elevation to the east. Of course there was nothing on it, except a few dust clouds far to the west from an old pickup making its way back to the Rez. The desert was flat and brown with scrubby mesquite and burned-out grass. Straight ahead across the border in Dos Piedras the Loma Prieta rose like a little pink knoll from among pitched hilltops. The clouds from last night's furious rainstorm had cleared and were now lumped like innocent rosy children above the hills. The shoulders of the tarred two-lane road were still wet and muddy where water had settled into depressions along the pavement.

Alejandra stopped at the intersection, listening to the Chevy's engine. It ran quietly and smoothly. Camayo knew cars and she never ceased to appreciate that about him. She gave it gas slowly, building up the RPM, but there wasn't a hitch or a tug or a false note. There was the trembling whine of immense power— a team of three hundred horses boosted to four by the customizing—ready to charge. She looked over the slick tar ahead, gauged the quarter mile and the half, set her stopwatch. She revved the engine, let out the clutch, and the Chevy leaped from the rear. Completely wired to the engine, Alejandra slipped into second gear at the perfect moment, and then round into third so nicely it hurt. She was laughing out loud when she broke her own record at the half mile.

Letting the Chevy find its own sweet balance, she continued with her planned trip to the border. In a mental notebook she marked the road surface and the ground around it, any curves or dips in the road. She'd transfer it all to paper later and confirm it over and over again.

The desert itself was the same everywhere—flat, sloping up in the unfathomable distance to tiny transparent blue peaks that seemed barely to exist. Reality was the sound of the engine, the throbbing of metal, the silken feel of primo leather and the steady stream of air passing the partially open window and brushing her cheek.

Sometimes the Loma Prieta settled into the ground and almost disappeared. Then it popped up again suddenly, or spun out from behind a hill as the road rose and fell and slid to either side. This shifting landscape was the only proof of the passing miles.

Sometimes—like today—she could almost forget about those weeks and months of torture. She felt the highway as though her body were the wheels experiencing every variation of surface and subtle change of temperature, but like the car, mechanically, without emotional response.

Before, it was the pain that kept her alive, only the pain and the grain of hope. But when they found the dismembered body in one of the excavation pits at Tyrex, her only thought had been God, if it's her, I'll hate you forever. After that, it was the anger...and still she hoped that somehow the jeans and sweatshirt, the high-top tennis shoes, even the leg, broken in two places in that fall from the giant slide—mi querida hija—that somehow it wasn't her. She denied it until the head was found, that pair of red barrettes still clinging to the brown curls.

There hadn't been a trial—not even an arrest. The mischievous dog carrying the skull he had dug up in the yard, prancing through the neighborhood in broad daylight, brought the police to the murderer's door. He killed one cop in the doorway before they shot him full of holes.

Her daughter, her fifteen-year-old Mariita, had still been afraid of men, even of the boys who came around wanting to take her to the drive-in, boys who always ended up talking cars with her mother. Boys with bulges in their tight pants. "Mama, it looks so big," Mariita kept saying, and Alejandra had laughed.

"When you're ready for it, it'll be the right size."

"No thanks," said Mariita, a show of mock horror on her face. "I'll never leave you, Mama."

"When you fall in love with a good man, we'll see," said Alejandra.

She still cried sometimes, but it was a wretched dry crying that gave no release, a crying wrung from her body, twisted like a rag caught beneath the wheels of a truck. At first, after Mariita was found, she still went to church. But she only went there to taunt God, to dare Him to do something else to her, anything. And that too had ended. Her eyes alone told the truth now, but she showed them only to the car mirror, and no one sat behind to see what that reflection said.

Alejandra slowed the car even more and just tooled along, drifting south, feeling like she was barely moving. The sun appeared brick red and explicit in the passenger window. The road ahead and the road behind swam like fire burning on water.

It was ten o'clock at night before Camayo finished with the Ford. As always when he was working on something of his own, he had been engrossed for hours, watching the pieces come together under the activity of his fingers. He turned off the lights, opened the garage door and stood leaning against the wall. It was cold, the air still wet from last night's storm. The stars shone like brilliant crystals and, in the immensity of their numbers, looked like they were falling to earth. Camayo felt the aching in his arms and shoulders, in his back and legs. His face was gritty with dirt and his fingers stiff. A hot cup of coffee and someone to talk to was what he needed. He sighed, then swore. He still saw Alejandra, although they didn't stay together anymore. They still worked together on cars, talked shop, and laughed sometimes. But she wasn't really there. He felt the absence of something he hadn't known was there until it wasn't. He kept coming back to that feeling, trying to find the right words for it. Shit, I just miss sacking her! But he knew that wasn't right either. She'd gone somewhere else when Mariita died, he knew with certainty, and he wished she'd come back.

But maybe that was asking too much. If only he could have done something to keep Mariita safe, even picking her up from school every day. But that was stupid. She was a teenager, with her own friends, and that maniac was watching and waiting to catch her alone. How could they know, oh God! He wanted to tell Alejandra these things, but he couldn't. What good would it do now?

Camayo scrubbed the grease from his hands with soft soap, then locked the garage and walked around the back to his house. The gate was standing open and he thought again about fixing it. As soon as this drag meet was over. And he had to try to talk to Alejandra too, he decided.

At this moment Alejandra was parked on the road a short distance away, leaning on the Chevy and staring morosely at the darkened garage. She had watched Camayo turn on the light above his front door. She imagined what he looked like, smelled like, the feel of his ratty T-shirt and the rough material of his Levi's. She wondered what it would feel like to touch his cheek again, feel his lumbering body against hers. But she could go no further. If she even tried, she would break. She had loved Ruben, yes, when the three of them had been together, the only family each had ever known. Now all I have left is the Chevy, she thought. The car that will take me to heaven...no, not heaven...that's where God is...but to where Mariita is.

Camayo washed himself in the shower. He could feel Alejandra someplace nearby. Maybe she was out there on the road, waiting for him. He knew how women were. They just wanted you to take those extra steps, go to them, and bring them back. They were afraid of things...he didn't know what. Stuff inside.

Afraid of a meteor falling on your head, yeah, that was real, but that nameless stuff? Then he thought about finding Mariita, how sick he'd been. How much he had dreaded seeing the guy who could have done it. Maybe even look in his eyes, a man like himself, but God, the sickness...Camayo folded the towel neatly on the rack. He still did things the way Alejandra had shown him. Why not? It worked best. Who wanted to come back to a wadded-up wet towel? Living alone and doing his own laundry, you thought of things like that. He was pulling on some clean pants when he heard the car engine. Shit! He grabbed a sweater and hopped to the door, trying to jam his feet into his boots. He pulled open the door and saw the taillights moving away, then the brake lights flashed and the car stopped. He heard the throaty gurgle of the idle. She had the window rolled down.

"You wanna come in?" he called. Pause. "You know—tacos tonight."

She didn't say anything.

"Why'd you stop then?" he asked. "You must have wanted something."

"Sit here. Sit with me a minute," she called to him, looking over her shoulder.

"Sure." He walked the fifty feet and got in. "Pull the car over, okay?...Just in case." She shifted into first carefully; the Chevy rumbled off the road.

He wanted to say, We may as well be sitting in the kitchen, but he didn't. He racked his brain. "I finished the Ford tonight. Lousy piece of shit!"

She laughed. "Sell it."

"Yeah, maybe. Come on, you wanna eat something?"

She knew he hadn't eaten. Neither had she. Maybe sitting at the kitchen table wouldn't be so bad.

"Then I gotta get some sleep. Been working nonstop," he said casually.

She knew what he was thinking. "Okay."

Alejandra watched Camayo at the stove, frying the meat, slicing the lettuce and tomato, grating longhorn. How long has it been since I cooked for him? Her mind went back to last spring, the barbecue, Mariita passing out the Cokes.

Penny for your thoughts, he wanted to say, but caught himself. None of their thoughts were safe. If she wanted to be quiet, okay. He took the tortillas out of the hot pan and filled them. He put all the tacos on a big plate in the center of the table and put the pot on for coffee. Then he went over and opened the screen door and called, "Hey! Carburetor!" A big black tabby with a white spot on one cheek ran inside, fixed Alejandra with a piercing look of recognition and walked over to his bowl. Camayo put some hamburger in it and the cat sat down, curled his tail around his haunches and started eating.

"Cabron!" said Camayo, laughing.

"Everything in its own time," said Alejandra.

"Yeah," he said and in the long silence he thought about how words often meant more than they said—even something way in the future, even something that already existed, only we didn't know about it. But then how did God figure out who got to suffer and who didn't? Innocent kids who'd never done anything bad to nobody? Was it just the luck of the draw? How could things be certain and uncertain at the same time? Wasn't there some rule by which it all worked? He thought again of the violated broken body of Mariita and pushed his plate away.

If Alejandra could have heard Camayo's thoughts, they would have surprised her. This was the guy whose world could only fit one way, with all the pieces the right ones. In fact, Camayo was thinking, if I do this or do that, a car will run better or worse. If I do this or that, the world will run better or worse. I don't care about the rest of the world, I just care about you. He would have said that, but since what happened to Mariita, he couldn't. He wondered why he couldn't make the pieces fit together anymore and then gave up. Maybe I just want to sack her.

Carburetor had eaten everything in his bowl and was sitting there purring, looking at them and waiting for more. No matter what happens, thought Camayo and Alejandra at the same time, he expects the best to happen. They caught each other looking at the cat and laughed.

"Come on, give him some more," said Alejandra.

"There isn't any more," said Camayo.

"So give him something else."

"I never get what I want, why should he?" said Camayo and instantly regretted it. "He's just a cat," he said.

"That's right," said Alejandra. "He's just a cat." She got up. "Thanks for the food." She stopped his reaction with her hand up. "No, really."

"You don't have to go," said Camayo. He was pissed now, following her to the door. "Just because of a damn cat!"

"Not because of the cat. Yes, because of the cat." She went out, not looking back at him, and he slammed the door after her. "Fuck!" He walked back into the kitchen and Carburetor ran into the other room to hide under the couch.

Alejandra didn't know she was crying until the headlights blurred on the road. "Why did I have to make such a big deal out of it? I should have ignored it. No, I can't. I just can't ignore anything anymore. Then how will I be able to live?" She didn't have an answer. The fact of her life or death remained there on the road in front of her; whatever the headlights showed, there was more darkness still ahead.

The day of the elimination drags went as everybody had expected. It came down to the necessary three—the Ford, the Chevy and an ugly green Dodge with chopped fenders that sounded like a nest of angry bees. "Stinger" was written on both doors of the Dodge and it was driven by a cowboy from Gila Bend. The rest of the drivers had come for the fiesta of it, lowriders from both sides of the border with zoot suits and lavishly painted cars, too shiny for anything but looking good. Everybody knew Camayo—and knew that the Chevy had been built by him too, so what did you expect? That the woman driving it benefited from her proximity to Camayo went without saying. They'd make the cowboy eat their exhaust. He'll wish he had stuck to horses, they laughed, spitting on the ground and drinking from their six-packs of Dos Equis. They surrounded the starting lanes at Camayo's garage for the first drag. There were three lanes starting, closing to two at the half mile where the drag was won or lost. Then all-out racing to the next drag point beginning at Cooney Road. Tomorrow there'd be a final all-out to the Shell station three miles this side of Two Rock.

Camayo knew what the Ford had and what the Chevy had. The Chevy could win, but could the driver win? That made it even. The Dodge didn't count. It would throw a rod the first day, he was sure of it. The cowboy had no finesse. He treated the Dodge like a steer he was roping and wrestling to the ground, not like a sensitive instrument that needed fine handling. Camayo went over to the Chevy. Alejandra was already in the car warming it.

"Well, good luck," he said, meaning it.

Her handshake was quick and hard. "You too."

You look a little pale, Camayo wanted to say, but that wouldn't be fair. He didn't feel that loose himself. The cowboy in the Dodge grinned and waved at them.

"Just remember, he'll try to push you to the outside, if he makes it that far." The Dodge had the center lane and would try to straddle the line at the half mile, he knew.

Alejandra nodded. She understood. It was always that way in drags, and it had happened to her before in the smaller events.

Merciless, Camayo thought, walking away. I have to be merciless, but he felt like a marshmallow. Just pretend there's nobody here but the Dodge. Alejandra was thinking the same thing: there's nobody here but the Dodge. The Dodge cowboy was thinking, there's nobody here but me. The cowboy knew the woman would be easy: he'd push her off the road at the half mile.

But what happened was this: the Chevy's nose came back off the shoulder in second gear and a car length later the Ford pushed in front and they pincered the Dodge between them without even planning it. It fell back, rocking heavily. The Chevy accelerated smoothly into third, as Camayo knew it would, and they traded noses twice, the Ford getting in front by its grillwork at Cooney Road.

Camayo came over to Alejandra afterward. He had intended to congratulate her for edging out the Dodge but when he saw how beat she was, he said instead, "You know, I never thought we'd be competing against each other. The way it was supposed to be, you'd take it to Cooney and I'd take it the rest of the way—with one car, the Chevy." All he could see was the woman, hollow-eyed and trembling from the strain. He was going to put his arm around her but she backed away from him.

"I'm not competing against you. It's for myself."

"Yeah, yeah. Look, you can still drop out. I'll drive the Chevy tomorrow—the cowboy doesn't stand a chance. And we can split the pot. Like it was supposed to be," he added.

"You mean we work on the cars together. You drive them and we share the pots..." She moved further away from him, trying to put the car between them. He followed her.

"Course it would make more sense if we were living together." He lowered his voice; he didn't want the whole world to hear him asking. She yanked open the car door and pulled her gym bag out, talking loud and mad, "Kind of late to start going macho on me, isn't it?"

"Well, women aren't too good at this part of it...driving, you know..." Damn it, he was trying to help her.

"You mean we don't go all out, run the car into the ground, risk our lives and other people's lives to win, that kind of thing?"

"It just isn't good for you." Now he was mad too, and before he could stop himself, he said, "It makes you hard."

She leaned against the Chevy for a minute, looking at him, and lifted her chin. "What are you really mad about, Camayo? That I didn't stay the other night? Well, go ahead, because I'm driving tomorrow." She walked past him without touching him.

"I'm not gonna make it easy for you next time," he called after her.

The next day the cowboy was staring straight ahead with a grim look on his face. Camayo grinned and waved. The cowboy nodded. Alejandra had a little smile but was staring straight ahead too. Time for the man to leave the little boy and girl behind. Time for a man's job. Camayo felt like he was in a movie he'd seen, with Tony Curtis playing a race car driver, but the girl had been in the stands where she belonged. Come on, knock it off. You know you'd rather have Alejandra right where she is instead of the stupid cowboy following you...but that's where she's gonna be, in the rear!

The Mexicans blew their horns. They wanted to rattle *everybody*. He heard the throaty voice of the Chevy beneath the whine of the Dodge, and somewhere between them, the super-rich confident roar of the Ford. The starter held his pink t-shirt up with both arms and brought it down. The sound was deafening. Beer cans flew into the air, spewing foam, and the bunched-up Ford leaped—what a gutsy little car—pleased and happy. He loved the Ford the best, let's face it. And all he knew at that moment was the clutch under his heel, the gearshift in his hand, the smell of rich gasoline and the sweat rolling down his chest. He realized that all he saw was the cherry red bulk of the Ford. Looking in the rear view mirror, he saw the Chevy and the Dodge fighting for the center lane, and then the wheels of the Dodge careened sideways off the road into the desert. A cloud of black smoke drifted up and blew apart in the wind.

"Cabron!" said Camayo, "No te dije? There goes his rod."

He didn't have time to think about it because the Chevy was on his tail. Alejandra looked as grim as old pennies. She came within an inch of his bumper before he edged the Ford away and into the first dip. He felt the suspension pull apart and come together again like a rubber band. The Ford barely dipped its nose and scooted out of the dip like a rabbit. The Chevy went in like a tank and came out like a tank. Then she crept up to the Ford like a high-powered vacuum cleaner and stayed there.

I taught her everything she knows but it's gotta stop somewhere. Confidence, not speed. He tensed his powerful arms and relaxed them. This was a test of superior skill and confidence. The Chevy's mine.

Alejandra moved to the inside, nicking the shoulder and sending a shower of mud over both cars. The Chevy sank into the road as though it were water. The road flowed under her, the car one with the coming depressions and curving of the land.

Camayo effectively blocked the Chevy on the inside again. That's how she'll come. She has no choice. The Ford's faster coming out. On the inside—she'll try to take me coming out.

Alejandra stuck to the inside until the last possible second, then let the Chevy glide as if it had sails lifting it above the ground. The car shuddered, trying to match wheels. Camayo jumped out of his seat as the Chevy appeared on his right. They were inside the dip fender to fender. He fought to hold the Ford as the road curved, but there was no place to go. The Chevy seemed to drift in slow motion, then slammed to the ground, frame rocking, sparks flying in a keening whine. He tried to close the Ford to the outside but it was too late. Camayo's mouth opened but nothing came out.

The rumble of the engine returned—to Alejandra as though a closed window was suddenly opened   I disappeared no not disappeared. I was floating off a cliff nothing to catch me, nothing—mas que el cielo the waters of her life falling toward her through silence...then she remembered her body being jolted as the Chevy screeched, sliced the muddy shoulder and the high-way, then glued itself to the tar again. The desert flooded back in, the sky was a mild blue with fans of clouds wisping up toward the sun. Mariita. The tears were wet on Alejandra's face, waters coursed through her body, streaming down the ready furrows of her earth to feed the hidden spring still underground.

She was holding a steaming cup of coffee, leaning on the hood of the Chevy at the Shell station when Camayo walked up.

"I don't care about the race. I only care about us," were the first words he spoke to her.

The Storyteller
With Nike Airs

By the time Lucia walked out of the Barrio, took the Greyhound bus de Tucson, changed buses in San Diego, changed again to the junky #10 bus to Santa Cruz, hung loose at the Metro with all the punks wearing purple and green hair, who looked more like los juveniles de sombra—the shadow kids—than they looked like themselves, took the Express to Watsonville, got off at the exit to Highway 152, trudged through the dunes, and arrived at a little wooden house sitting in the middle of a stinking brussels sprout field, the women were already crying.

The field worker and the cannery worker were there; the woman from town who worked at the Nopalitos Restaurant was there too. La doctora from the clinica had been there, trying to do something, but there was no point. The patient had not responded to any of her treatments.

Having been raised in a family of folk healers, la doctora trusted her instincts. There was nothing physically wrong with Josefina; it was a spiritual illness, what the old people called daño, the kind of soul damage better left to a curandera to deal with. At least for now, la doctora decided, because—and here her modern medical training obscured her vision—Josefina was not in any life-threatening situation.

The women who were crying knew better. La doctora was right about one thing, though: la curandera alone understood the true nature of the illness. Josefina didn't want to keep breathing because the world she had come to inhabit was a world without life. It was a life in which the earth, La Madre de todos, was dead, or more correctly in Josefina's understanding, La Madre had been murdered. The desert, with its birds and animals and cactus flowers, had retreated all the way to the mountains. She couldn't reach it. To go on living was impossible. The pain was unbearable, and Josefina spun off into imaginary landscapes confirming her perception that the desert was gone, and she was lost, a wanderer through the fields of an alien world.

While the other women were weeping, la curandera was sitting quietly and intently beside Josefina. But she was thinking, La cosa es, Josefina tiene razon. Her desert belongs to the rich, and the day when there is no place left for her fell on her head. Y aqui, la esclava de los files no tiene fin. She can't escape the labor of the fields here, and she has no strength. She is swallowed up. Only one chance is left: Lucia has to make a place for Josefina's life and plant her in it.

That her godchild could accomplish this feat of story telling, la curandera never doubted. Wasn't she the cream of all her students? Hummph! And the one who gave her the most grey hairs too. Lucia's seventeen years were too few for her daring, but there was no time in this world to dance barefoot or sit fanning oneself under a tree. Lucia would have to go through many trials, and it hurt la curandera's heart that she would not be there to help. For that reason, she reminded herself, she had to be strong with Lucia while she could.

So, when Lucia came through the door, la curandera said, quite gruffly, "Hasta que llegastes, it's about time you got here! Ponte fuerte, the matter is urgent!" She gave Lucia a glass of rainwater, blessed by her hand, to drink, and that was all.

The three women stopped sniffling and listened intently. They had never seen or heard a storyteller like Lucia before: a kid with beads hanging in strings from her feathered hair, Levi's with holes in the knees and a faded black leather jacket, and—even more scandalous—pink and lavender high-top tennies with fluorescent green laces.

Lucia laughed, "Chill out, nina!" The women drew in their breath, but Lucia was deep in her teacher's eyes, inside that jolt of recognition that told her who she was. In that moment, Lucia saw her own mother's words from so long ago, carrying the seed of a world inside. "Desde chiquita anda haciendo cuentos. All she does is make stories, but now she's disappearing inside of them. La cosa es serio. Do what you can with her and teach her whatever she can learn." So saying, her mother gave ten-year-old Lucia into the hands of her nina. La curandera began explaining to Lucia the nature of words, how to use them to make a world. And how to bring sick people back to their bodies.

And this was what Lucia was here for now. Her nina was right: Josefina looked deader than dead. Without wasting another second, Lucia started her breath deep in her stomach, clearing the path from heart to head and emptying her body so it could contain only a deep yearning, a desire, a vast and impersonal love needed to make the way to reach Josefina.

When Lucia was prepared, la curandera had covered the windows and turned to her. "Now, remember what I taught you. Don't be in a hurry and you won't get lost. No mas, don't stop to hang out at the corner con los juveniles deliquentes, because those shadow kids can make you forget. Your body just sits here and rots if you forget everything."

"Ya, ya, nina," said Lucia. "They're just kids." Here she was, wrecked from traveling all night, and starving, but she couldn't eat anything because it would cloud her body and she wouldn't be able to see clearly. And her nina was already beginning.

First, la curandera placed her hands on Josefina, one at the top of her spine and one at the bottom, letting her own life force circulate through Josefina's body. After some minutes she removed her hands and poured cold water over them up to the elbows. Then the woman from the Nopalitos Restaurant made a circle around Josefina with yerba buena, and she and the other two sat outside it at three points, guarding it. Lucia and la curandera sat inside the circle with the patient.

Lucia felt her everyday self, the rad kid from the Barrio, begin to fade into the background. She knew where to go to open the channel to her power. As fast as an intention, she was back home in the desert, climbing quickly up the eastern mountains above Gate's Pass. As she drew near, the rocky slope turned purple, and in the circle of her personal sacred place the jumping cactus stood in clumps, golden and haloed by the rising sun. Pinpoints of light from a deep pool of water danced like stars in her eyes. She surrendered her fears to the mountain, knowing it would keep her strong, and brought herself, the self with no name, back to the circle.

La curandera was holding the grounding healing energy steady, and Lucia-with-no-name began to listen to Josefina's body. She saw the story the woman's body was telling, and gradually the room faded. All of a sudden Lucia left the circle with a "pop" and was inside Josefina's story, tracking her:

Josefina saw her brothers riding horses at full gallop toward the village and recognized a friend, the boy she'll marry someday, but his face seemed to change as he drew near. When he pulled up the reins in front of her, it wasn't him. The air was filled with angry sweating faces and hoarse shouts and the glint of sunlight on steel.

Josefina tried to run, but she was in an abandoned house which suddenly filled up with young white men fixing things. She realized there was no one there, and she was in a room with walls heating up like the metal insides of a stove. She glanced frantically around the kitchen for something recognizable, but there were only things, white metal things that made buzzing and grumbling noises.

Amid the clutter of old take-out boxes, rotting food and garbage, a baby sat alone in a highchair made out of ironwood. Where there had been a wall only a moment before, there were multiple panes of glass. On the roof of the garage next door she saw the gringo boys with their dogs, black huskies all with the exact same markings. They were milling around in the tight area of the roof, and below them water was backed up and smelled like a sewer.

Josefina ran back through the house, the baby in her arms...but no, the baby wasn't in her arms anymore. She didn't know where she herself was, on the street, circling buildings in a panic. She finally saw the boys on the roof, and one of them told her the names of streets, but they were incomprehensible to her. She saw so many jagged streets and crooked houses, but she couldn't tell what they looked like; they were shining so brightly with a blackish shine, like fresh tar...not fresh tar...blood, as black as the water of a lagoon.

Then the train appeared in front of her, standing still, so huge and shining with the same black light, without a sound, motionless and waiting. Josefina walked toward a kind of subway entrance, where a group of schoolgirls stood. She tried to speak their language, but the girls couldn't make sense of what she was saying and quickly lost interest. Just as they were scattering, she thought of the right question to ask, "What place is this? What part?" They were unfamiliar with directions, they conferred. "East, yes, east," one affirmed. Then Josefina saw the land beyond, geometrical, a pattern of unfamiliar shades of green and blue separated by grey or black stripes rolling up and down slick rubbery-looking hills. There were vermilion squares, like linoleum, and red rocks everywhere. Suddenly she knew what was on the hill: a saguaro without any arms, a bare trunk coated in teflon standing in a circle of fake rocks that gleamed like glass. Josefina screamed but she didn't know at what; the village, the earth and the bluepurpleyellowgreen of her homeland blew up in front of her like from the explosion of a bomb. It knocked her on her face. Her teeth were gritty with dust and someone was pressing her down. She held the baby, shielding it with her body. With a shock, she saw the baby's open eyes were blue, a strange flat blue without luster. But she knew it was alive; she felt its beating heart against her breast.

The muscles of Josefina's back jumped convulsively, bare flesh being cut with a razor. Systematically, deliberately, the soldier's blade slashed letters into her back, and then continued, making a cut like a half moon around the baby's eye with the sharp tip of the blade. Neither Josefina nor the baby made a sound, and there was no blood.

But the train loomed above her, wet and glistening black as though it had passed through dying entrails. The teflon desert stretched in front of her, black lines dissecting it in all directions, but there was no blood there either. Josefina heard her own voice, as though her consciousness was burning in a final blazing fire, bright enough to make words: "Si asi es, no quiero vivir!"

She spun off from her life into a place that was freezing cold and buried in silence. The only thing she saw, reflected back at her out of the darkness, was her own eyes, and those eyes were blue.

Lucia-with-no-name, tracking Josefina's story as it developed, reached this point just as Josefina disappeared into the jumbled-up streets behind the subway. Lucia had been able to interpret the varying landscapes of Josefina's story correctly, although their jagged edges pierced one another like a broken puzzle of glass. The pieces Josefina had left behind would soon fade without her energy, and Lucia was pissed at herself for not getting there before Josefina had created the teflon desert—that was what took her off the deep end. But God, the train was something else!

Lucia walked around the giant glittering train but it faded out in back, incompletely imaged, like the false fronts at Old Tucson. Still, it was pretty rad for an old lady.

Now Josefina had entered a place of bits and pieces of unreal stories floating in fantasy, without souls. She would be harder to find; it would be harder to sift out the stray sentences and words—or even just letters—to find her.

Thinking of the pale blue eyes she'd seen, and the bloodless wounds, Lucia knew there wasn't much time. Then she saw las juveniles de sombra across the street, flickering on and off. Boy, they wanted to live badly, clinging to the wisps of Josefina's story with what rays they had. The shadow kids were soul punks, souvenirs of every living person's growing-up. They populated the corners of all the stories Lucia had been in. Sometimes they were nice; sometimes they were as mean as cactus thorns in your heel. They weren't important to a story, just fixtures of memory, but sometimes they could make a story or break it.

Lucia-with-no-name took a deep breath: this was one of those times. She had run out of clues; maybe they knew where Josefina was.

Lucia sauntered across the street, flashing her lavender and pink Nike Airs. The shadow girls, one wearing Josefina's huaraches, watched Lucia coming with ravenous envy. Desire-to-have leaped out of them in sickening green ooze that barely missed Lucia's feet. The strongest of them, a concoction of the most sangrona bully at school and the sonza who would break your head with the bat for striking her out, leaned toward Lucia out of a vat of something that looked like the swirling Orange Julius sold on South Sixth in the summer. She glared at Lucia and said, "Dame tus Nikes or I'll make you wish you never set foot en Watsonville!"

Pretty smart, thought Lucia, and her estimation of Josefina's creativity went up another notch. As she was thinking about it, she felt her nina yank on the string tying them together—a hard yank that clearly said, "Quit messing around y sigue con el cuento because Josefina's vibes are getting weaker."

Lucia felt a gust of snow beginning to fall in the Sierras and she knew with certainty that Josefina had gone beyond words and was going where neither of them had any business going. The story signs were turning into scratches and mere punctuation marks fluttering in the wind. Only ghosts of memories wandered there, unable to come home. They could all be lost, even the women guarding the circle.

Lucia thought quickly. "Listen," she said, snagging a green streak from the lead shadow girl with her fingernail, "I'll give you my Nikes if you tell me where Josefina is."

"Who?" sneered the lead shadow kid, disdain gleaming in her eye. Lucia was having a tough time following the eye as it twirled around.

"You know who: the reason you have any shoes at all."

The shadow kid's mouth flopped over in a smirk, but the smirk vanished when Lucia took off her Nike Airs and dangled them by their fluorescent green laces.

"Take the old way to the valley," the shadow kid said respectfully. "Then across on the edge of Wolf Ridge. She's in a clump of pines." Lucia handed over the Nikes and the shadow leader, with this added strength, sucked the other shadow girls in with a smack.

Awesome, thought Lucia-with-no-name, pero no vale nada. At least I hope not. She pulled the threads of the story in, tied them to her wrist, and made the words that dropped her on the expert run at Squaw Valley at the edge of darkness. Bitter ragged snow flurries raked her face from the storm level blowing off the ridge. Lucia made up a ton of ski lessons and snapped her boots into a new pair of Rossignol 180s.

"Sierra winter sucks!" growled Lucia. "How the heck does this transplanted India refugee from the desert know this stuff?"

"Good intuition," she felt her nina say through morse coded yanks on their common strings.

"Good thing I read nina's book *Skiing The Killy Way* last year when I was sick."

Lucia pushed off toward a black maw of howling snowstorm. No more cow pucky, meadow muffin crap, she thought. This is it. I've got to get her now or *las tortillas se comen el suelo mugroso!* The tortillas bite the caca floor!

Meanwhile, in the brussels sprout field on the central coast of California, the little house was shaking like a 5.5. The ping ping of phantom hailstones hit the roof and slid down like clanking chains against the sides of the house. The wallboards creaked and a roar of wind turned into the snuffling slobbering snarl of some gigantic animal trying to eat through the house.

The daño in Josefina's soul, knowing its time was limited, was trying to break into the world. There was a scratching on glass, over and over again, like a blade writing on the window, trying to make the words that would split it open. La curandera cautioned the three women guarding the circle with her eyes, and they held tight, shaking in their calzones with fright.

Back in the Sierras above Squaw Valley, Lucia was struggling to reach Josefina before they both went off the edge of the story into a crevice of pain from which no one would return. Following the steps her spiritual mother taught her, Lucia-with-no-name walked, or rather, skied on the side of nothing, where threads of many stories, living or without soul, drifted like snakes without skins. At last she dropped down on Josefina squatting beneath a gondola, her past and her blank future hanging above her head in the heavy air.

Not bothering with a greeting, Lucia wove her own story into Josefina's. A bubble of warm air expanded around them, a microcosm of Lucia's sacred place. Outside the snow was a blinding fury, but inside the smell of sage mingled with the perfume of wild honeysuckle. Lucia plunged Josefina with her into the desert pool of spring-fed waters, and they floated.

Although she couldn't speak, Josefina's eyes were dark again and her skin warm to the touch. The scars on her back bled at last (the way they had that day the Mexican soldiers destroyed her village). In the water the blood changed to sparks and passed through both of them, as if they were made of air.

When Josefina emerged from the water she saw what was really there: Lucia and the living force of the desert surrounding her life. Lucia drew Josefina into the circle, showing her how to enter and leave, so she could keep this piece of wild desert of the heart to last forever. It would be a place she could go to and be at peace, a real place.

Lucia-with-no-name pulled the ends of their stories tight and put the slack between her teeth. For added insurance, she tied Josefina to her with a string dipped in honey. Then she ended the story with a sound like the whirring of great wings—clearly a convention of her own—and shot back into the little house with a snap so hard the furniture rattled.

A few moments prior, la curandera had lit her sweet grass pipe and was quickly blowing mouthfuls of smoke in all directions, not knowing where they would pop in from. The storyteller, Lucia-with-no-name, arrived coughing madly, waving her arms to clear the smoke. She dumped Josefina unceremoniously into her body. Then she told the guards to open the door. As soon as Josefina opened her eyes, la curandera made her close them again and suggested a deep and peaceful sleep.

"Hasta que llegastes!" her nina exclaimed to Lucia, who had pulled in all of herself from the sacred place and was grinning ear to ear.

"Se te paro el pelo, didn't it?" she laughed at her nina. La curandera's hair had come loose from her hairpins, her long black skirt was turned sideways and her glasses slid down to the edge of her nose. Then Lucia understood, and kissed her nina's wrinkled cheek. "It's okay, I'm okay, nina," she said softly.

"Ya ya, quitate," said her nina with fake gruffness. La curandera dissolved the gathering and sent the guards home. She made almond tea for Lucia and drank a Carta Blanca Dark herself. The old woman and the young woman went outside and had a good laugh. They laughed until their nervous systems had shaken out all the ghost words.

Her nina took out a piece of licorice stick she had in her pocket and gave it to Lucia, who nibbled it, then leaned back comfortably against the wall of the little house and went to sleep in the evening sun.

"She might be a great storyteller some day," mumbled Lucia's nina to herself, "if she would only learn to stop wearing her good shoes to work." La curandera was looking at Lucia's Nike Airs, covered all over with green, shiny, slimy goop.

The Pan Birote

Nobody wanted to get up early and wash with cold water just because it was Sunday and they had to go to church. All over the Barrio, kids were trying to get away from equally determined mamas who were torturing them with wet smelly cloths and big-toothed combs that tore out their hair along with the knots.

El Güero y el Prieto were already cranky because the afternoon before they had gotten the mean Father for confession and had to tell him all their bad words, bad thoughts and bad actions. Who knew if a bad word was said fifty-eight or a hundred times since last week? And was it their fault if the other boys wanted to run en bola past the girls on the way home from school and grab their nalgas? And how couldn't they have wanted the same thing even if they hadn't actually done it? The Father punished them as though they had done the bad stuff too; the darn mean priest made them say so many Our Fathers and Hail Marys that they were still in the church after all their smirking friends had left and it was dark when they came out. They had to run all the way home chased by espantos!

As soon as they got free of Abuelita's hands, the boys were outside fighting and throwing dirt at each other. Abuelita yelled at them, "No dejan ni alistarse! En lugar de dar gracias a Dios estan peleando en dia de misa? Ya veran...! I can't even get ready in peace! Just wait till I get you!" she threatened. She was old; their grandmother not their mother, but she had to be mother and father and everything, without rest.

At last the old lady was ready along with that brat, Chiltepin, who had to have her braids done every morning. After Abuelita had corralled them all into the kitchen for inspection they set out, Abuelita dragging Chiltepin by the hand and the boys following behind, shoving and hitting each other every chance they got. They had just invented a game out of kicking rocks when Abuelita yelled at them to stop wearing out their shoes. They ran around, itchy and hot in their wool suits, tagging each other just to get away from her eyes for even a second. Abuelita made one more appeal to God to give her paciencia and walked faster.

It was difficult to feed and care for three children who acted como el demonio and assaulted life without thinking of the consequences. And this Sunday the whole world would be there to get the pan para los pobres, the bread for the poor. This was why she was going to this church so far away—watching for alacranes and viboras at every step. Los niños acted como si no tuvieran ojos, as if they were blind!

Abuelita looked forward to those moments in God's presence when she could rest and believe in His ultimate plan for her. The children didn't have these expectations. They lived the cruel reality of the moment, but with the grace of the child who looked with bright new eyes at each day. So they did not yet suffer as she did, watching the years go by without being able to make things better and feeling guilty for everything that went wrong.

"Ay, Dios mio, ayudame, God help me!" She tightened her grip on little Chiltepin's hand. She had to get bread for these hungry mouths even if it meant going to High Mass. Everyone would be dressed to the teeth y iban a hacer malas caras at her rundown shoes, which she had cleaned with water, and her common dress. Everyone would look down their noses at her. Well, que coman caca, she reasoned. Bread was bread, and the children had to eat. She was going to church this time, even if she had nothing good to wear. Her dress was clean, and that was that.

When they got there the church was already crowded, the men lining up behind the pews in back. No, se iban a morir de calor if they stayed there. It was too hot so she pushed her three children ahead and squeezed them into an already full pew near the front. The boys immediately saw that the Sisters were all sitting across the aisle. They could see the hooked nose of "La Mala" poking out from her habit. She would be glaring knives at them if they said one word, and to heck with that! So right away they said, "Ma, we want to sit in back." "Callense! Shut up!" said

Abuelita and made them sit down. They wriggled and sat on Chiltepin until they pushed her out and got the aisle space, where there was a little more room, for themselves. Chiltepin hated it up front because everybody acted like she could sit down on one inch just because she was little, and she couldn't see anything either. She tried to squat down behind the footrest, but Abuelita told her to cover her calzones and sit up like a girl.

This was not only el dia de pan para los pobres, but the Archbishop was visiting so the boys knew all the Sisters would have ants in their pants and find ways to punish them at school for how they acted in church. Already the mean one had noticed them. Her eyes were glued to them and her stiff pale face was glowing in anticipation of slamming a yardstick against their butts. So el Güero y el Prieto knelt down and stared at their dirty knuckles, gritting their teeth so they wouldn't start laughing or "La Mala" would drag them out from the pew in front of everybody. Chiltepin jammed herself in between Abuelita and a gorda, a big fat woman with red nails and rings on her fingers who ignored the child and took up all the kneeling space.

The high mass was longer than ordinary mass, and it looked like they put in more stuff because of the Archbishop. There were four Fathers at the altar with him, dressed in their gold robes. Everybody was wound tight with pride, that they were having communion on this important day, and with fear that they wouldn't get through the mass without mishap because it was so hot and crowded and they were starving. Getting up and down and kneeling and sitting, back and forth, with rapidly beating hearts and dry mouths, la gente tried hard to concentrate on the holy mass. Their stomachs rumbled like freight trains and they coughed to cover it up, so everyone sounded like they had tuberculosis.

The hunger of the cathedral full of gente was a tangible thing. It quickly made itself into a giant straining entity reaching out to engulf the altar and finish the mass so it could get at the bread. The attending Padres felt it and glared out at la gente with narrowed eyes, daring them to be inattentive. So they shifted each guilty nalga gingerly, one at a time, hanging from the edge of their seats and staring at their libros de misa with serious faces but not seeing a thing. Ruffling the pages for no reason, they gazed around at the walls during the reading of the Epistle, unable to understand the Archbishop's fractured Spanish pronunciation. Then they mumbled along with the Latin parts. There was a sudden wakeful silence when they heard the priest say, "And those are the words of the Holy Gospel, amen." After that, the Padres went through the offering of the chalice, the Pater Noster and the passing out of the host with swift determination.

The people receiving communion had not drunk even a drop of water since the night before, and the host stuck to the roofs of their mouths. For the innocent, there was always the possibility of panic, wondering if they were going to choke on the body of Our Lord and fall down and crack their heads on the marble floor. Trying in vain to swallow, and not daring to bite down on it, the boys contorted their faces and finally got their tongue to roll the wafer into a little ball and balanced it while scurrying back to their seats, hands clasped in front of them. They then worked the little balls of dough around in their mouths until they found the saliva to swallow them. They were in a hurry for the mass to be over so they could eat the bread, the sooner the better.

The Archbishop shouted out the prayers following communion with grand authority, and the people, chastised, beat their breasts with fervor, especially the children because this was a chance to redeem themselves and feel sorry for all their greedy feelings. But all of them were secretly inching toward the end of their pews, getting into position for the charge to the altar rail for the bread.

From under lowered eyelids and squinted eyes, they observed the helpers bringing out the huge cardboard boxes from the sacristy. After one taut second of forced decorum, the entire mob surged forward, pushing and pulling the little ones in front so the number of hungry mouths could be counted. Those who got their loaves fought their way outside, skipping down the wide steps and barely dashing around the corner before ripping open the soft, fragrant, tantalizing pan birote. This was a moment for all stomachs to expand. But Abuelita was strict with her ideas—she wouldn't let her family start eating its loaves in the street. But to stop their chillando, she told them they would have the responsibility of carrying the two loaves of pan birote home safely.

It must be said, to their credit, that the family was more than halfway home before the two boys started to drift behind. Los dos gallitos, uno güero y uno prieto, pero los dos de sangre de jalapeño, roosters with jalapeño juice for blood, were grinning for one reason only: the pan birote was feeling like a captured warm-breasted chickadee in their little hands.

Ya venian mugrosos. They were filthy from the hot sun and the desert remolinos that showered them with dust more than once, but the thrill of inspiration was making their hearts beat faster. They were hungry now, and besides, a little dirty area which no one would want to eat anyway had appeared on one end of the pan. So el Güero, with the authority of the oldest, pinched and twisted off one end of the pan birote along with the surrounding area and popped it into his mouth. El Prieto followed with his loaf. The crisp golden end appeared for one instant only between his shining white teeth. Flushed with the success of their initial acts, and with stomachs alert and pleading for more, it was a foregone conclusion that the soft, luminescent, innermost center of the pan birote swiftly appeared. The contrast of pure white against the brown of their hands and the dark blue material of their coats had the power of a beautiful painting.

This is what Chiltepin saw when she twisted her head around to check on the continued existence of the pan. Just as she turned, the boys tore off large chunks and, giggling and shoving each other in encouragement, stuffed them into their mouths. Seeing this scandalous activity taking place a few feet behind and aware that she was still a vast distance from the kitchen table and the just apportionment of the pan birote, she yanked hard on Abuelita's hand, crying, "Ma! Ma! The pan birote, they're *eating* it!" But to her dismay and complete incomprehension, Abuelita did not even turn around. She merely responded in an angry voice, "Andan, cabrones! No les pagues atencion! Just stop looking at them!"

Nearly frantic over the rapidly diminishing pan birote, Chiltepin tried to get free from the hand keeping her from the bread, but Abuelita wouldn't let go. She was forced to gallop along in anger and despair, hearing the guilty but triumphant laughter behind and the increasing volume of chomping teeth. She could not understand why Abuelita wasn't doing anything about it, why she was being told to play the part of the hungry but proud: these things were nothing compared with the desire to get her share. In spite of her unequal age and sex, deep in her blood she knew the meaning of equality. *She* was hungry and *she* had a right to eat too. And this had nothing to do with who was bigger or better.

The sun beating down on the long walk to and from church, the fasting ordeal already endured, and the insult to her stomach from the long–awaited pan birote that was in danger of never arriving—the bitter injustice of these things—was too much, and she finally twisted her hand free.

"You better give me some," she said, turning around, barely keeping the quiver of a six–year–old from her voice.

"Oh yeah? And what are you going to do about it if I don't?" mocked el Güero. The younger boy, ashamed but a conspirator, said nothing. They kept walking, holding aloft the pan birote and tearing off pieces with predator teeth.

"If you don't, I'll spit on it!" She was advancing beside Abuelita while walking backward.

"You do and you won't have a mouth left," the oldest said.

"Maaa!" she wailed. "They're eating all the bread."

With a stiff back, Abuelita repeated, "Dejalos, cabrones. Forget it. Ya que lo manosearon todo, que se lo coman! Now that they got it all dirty, they can have it!"

"Why do they get to eat it and I don't?"

"Porque asi son los hombres, that's how men are." She walked faster. Chiltepin had to run to keep up.

"I don't care. You said we could eat it when we got home!"

"Pues, ya ves, asi es el mundo, that's life."

"No!" She ran back. Her tormentors committed the final sacrilege of tossing the last loaf back and forth between them out of her reach. Facing them and planting her feet, she screamed, "I want it! I want it! Give it to me!"

"Here, you stupid crybaby," said the oldest, tearing off a hunk and throwing it at her. She was picking it up when he shoved her.

"Leave her alone," el Prieto said then. "Let her eat it."

She ran to Abuelita, happily dividing her piece. "Here, Ma." She held up the fragment.

"No. No quiero."

"Come on, Ma, it's for you."

Abuelita looked down and then carefully took the offered crust and bit off a tiny piece. "Ya no necesito mas. That's all I want."

So, straggling behind, los dos jalapeños ate the remainder of their pan birote down to the last crumbs on their identical blue suits. And Chiltepin, rejoicing in the fruits of her struggle, nibbled the wonderful pan birote with her strong baby teeth all the rest of the way home.

Adonde Vive Dios?

Lupe Reyes' fingers moved constantly, going around and around each of the beads as she repeated her oracion, painfully, earnestly, moving her lips along with the prayers. The haphazardly curtained windows of shacks like hers spoke of emptiness and hunger and the kind of despair that comes only after honest effort results in nothing but failure. The abandoned lives within the gouged walls—the dry, splintering wooden doors—breathed only endings. Nothing new could be born from these people's hearts. Even endurance seemed like a sin here, obscene, rotting.

Only Lupe Reyes still believed in miracles. Because she deserved a miracle. She deserved to have God reveal Himself to her.

Hadn't He promised...she didn't know what...but surely his be-
lievers—the doers of all the things He ordered—could at least
expect, and receive, mercy. Mercy in the form of recognition.
Recognition that would bring just one little act of vengeance on
all the evildoers and, it goes without saying, a little something for
the others to enjoy—to stretch out over—after all the diligence, all
the paying attention to His will.

Otherwise, what was all the pain for?

Lupe Reyes left the candle burning. In the dark, it was something to look at. It gave her eyes something to do, following the
flickering golden light as it cut the darkness, filled the bare walls
and empty corners. So she was not so alone. And then she slept.
The walls were grey, the candle fluttering in a yellow puddle,
when she opened her eyes again. Except for that, nothing had
changed. She sighed, kissed the crucifix on the rosary around her
neck, and got up. It was harder to do each day, pero, ay Dios dira.
She went out and dumped the can of piss in the ravine behind the
shack and then washed her hands with a cup of water from the
close to empty bottle. She'd have to take the bottle to the gas station at the fork, or better the other one, the one way down at La
Quinta—she hadn't been there lately—to get water from their hose.
If there was nothing to eat that morning...pues, her panza was
getting too big anyway.

When she got to the gas station, el gringo dueño was there.
She watched from behind a clump of saguaros across the road,
her tapalo covering her face to keep away the moscas that were
eating the dog shit a few feet away. She waited and watched, and
when she didn't see him for a while, she walked over gingerly and

started filling her bottle. She was almost done when, anda cabron, there he came from around the back, carrying a dirt-covered tire in each hand. When he saw her he started yelling. She let the hose go and tried to run, but the water bottle was too heavy and it almost slipped from her fingers. The maldito let the tires roll and, picking up the hose, aimed it at her back. The water was like the shock of a fist striking her shoulders. The fat pig of a dueño squealed with loud phlegm-filled laughter. When she heard him coughing and spitting she looked back and saw the hose snaking in his hands and the water going all over his feet. "Anda, se lo pago Dios," said Lupe Reyes, satisfied. After that the bottle did not seem so heavy, nor the way so long. She cut through the mesquites near Obregon and stopped to pick some quelites that had sprouted in the shallow ditch beneath some trees. There were even some nice verdolagas creeping along the rocky ground: what a nice tangy flavor they would add to the quelites. Holding her mantle with the greens to her breast, she followed the trail across Obregon. Dust covered her huaraches, and when she got home she used a few precious drops of water to wash and cool her feet. When Jesus had washed the disciples' feet it was not only humility, she knew. After all, if He expected them to walk so far, He had to show them how to take care of their feet. Then she went down to the arroyo and gathered a few pieces of wood brought down by the flash floods. She used one of the matches in the librito from the diner at the crossroads. Quintero, the bartender, was her friend. He always said to take as many as she needed. But she never took more than two books at a time. So he would see she was careful. She looked, like she always did, at the picture on the matchbook. A young and beautiful naked woman with nothing but stars on her chee-chees, who bent over nicely so one could light the match on her nalgas. Hombres cochinos, she thought, like she always did, then folded the matchbook and put it safely away in the empty can by the comal.

After she had eaten the quelites and verdolagas, it was not so hard. She could believe again that she would live through this day too, and that a miracle was coming soon. It was descending from the skies, from God's favorite place, the one just between the peaks that always looked golden and glowing with a special light, like la Virgencita's cheek above the stand of candles. Then this miracle would skim the lomitas, gathering force as it came speeding over the boulders, flying down the sandy wash like a sudden flash flood on an August afternoon. And when it reached her jacal this miracle would burst open, absorbing the land, the house, and her in it, in one stupendous cataclysmic light that would transform everything forever. And then what? She didn't know, except that she would never be alone again and her life would cease to be painful. The aging woman in a ragged black dress, with calloused tired feet, fingers distorted by labor, crooked teeth with more spaces than teeth and deep sorrowful eyes that, nonetheless, took joy in seeing; with a strong body that slept and woke, that moved and yearned to rest: this whole mujer would rush toward heaven, pulled by an ecstasy of recognition, with total forgiveness, total love, and—somehow—she would never experience her old life in this world again; and—somehow—she would be alive forever. That was what God promised; that was the miracle she waited for, knew would come, had to come. God would not disappoint her. She only had to wait long enough.

But her friend, old Señora Quiroz, who lived some ways west and beyond the arroyo, did not see things this way. "Gozar de la vida," is what Señora Quiroz always said. But it was easy for her to do, who had a big healthy grandson coming around with bags of groceries. Of course, that was nice for Lupe Reyes too, because then Señora Quiroz would come to the edge of the gully and call, "Lupita, Lupita, ven a tomar cafecito conmigo," and there was always sugar in it too, and Señora Quiroz never let her leave with empty hands. "Mira, Lupita," Señora Quiroz would always say, as they sat on orange crates under the ramada, noisily sipping the hot black cafe with pleasure, "Mira, Lupita, what you need to do is find yourself a man, un buen hombre."

"Callate, Carmelita," Lupe Reyes would say, "What do I need a man for? Y ya sabes that with a man around, miracles never come close."

"Ay, tu y tus miracles," Señora Quiroz would scoff, "Miracles are not as good as flesh and bone, ever."

"The solace of the flesh is gone for me forever," said Lupe Reyes. "From now on until God takes me, I know nothing of the flesh."

"A big strong woman like you?" said Señora Quiroz, but she knew better than to continue. She'd have to go visit Maria Tiburon down on La Cinquenta if she wanted to discuss pleasure, and that was a long walk away.

"My miracle is on its way. I know it," said Lupe Reyes, getting that bright streak in her dark eyes again. "I feel it right here in my heart. But I promise—when it comes I won't go without saying adios."

"No, ningunos adioses quiero yo!" Señora Quiroz snapped petulantly. The very idea that Lupe would be going anywhere, leaving her behind, was unspeakable. She refused to even consider it.

Lupe Reyes smiled, remembering this most recent conversation with old Señora Quiroz. Then she got up and went to the arroyo to wash her dishes with sand. When she was finished, she went on sitting there. She wasn't just sitting but she wasn't exactly looking or listening to anything. It was more like watching and waiting. And not that either: like making an agreement of some kind, to be a certain thing, a person of substance, but without a name, without identification, just Lupe-with-sand-between-her-toes, or Lupe-with-sun-on-her-skin. And between one breath and the next, she wasn't even that.

Suddenly the arroyo was on fire. The mesquites along the banks of the arroyo were burning. The sand exploded into diamonds in front of her eyes. And then she felt a cool breeze lift the hair from her forehead, and she felt herself breathing, just like always, felt the rocks under her feet, and she thought she heard her name. It was. It was Señora Quiroz's voice sounding far away.

"Lupita, Lupita, ayudame! Lupita," the voice called again. Lupe Reyes stood up quickly, looking this way and that down the arroyo. There was nothing to be seen.

"Carmelita! Señora Quiroz!" she called, and waited, but there was no sound. Nothing. Suddenly terror gripped her heart. Without going to find her huaraches, she went hurriedly down the arroyo, trying to step in the soft sand between the rocks and boulders. As she climbed up to the trail that left the arroyo and went south, the thorny branches of a paloverde lifted the tapalo from her head, but she didn't stop to untangle it. She left it stuck on the tree, a black piece of cloth, and went as quickly as she could through the grove of barrel cactus to the old horse path from Rancho Acequia. Margaritas still bloomed there, now gone wild, among the cholla and tall grass. Now that the way was free, she almost ran in the soft cool dirt of the horse path until she reached Los Portales. From the broken-down gates, she could see down the slope to Señora Quiroz's shack. It sat next to a vast piece of open ground that had once been the rancho's grazing land, now peppered with loco weed and wild grass rippling in the wind.

There was no sign of life. No smoke came from the comal. The palm branches that made up the ramada roof lifted here and there as the winds blew, and somewhere metal clanged against metal.

"Carmelita, adonde estas?" Lupe called, descending the slope. No one answered. She reached the door out of breath. She tried it, expecting to find it locked, but the door flew open and banged against the wall. Frightened, she looked quickly inside the small room, but it was dark—the windows were still covered— and there was nothing to be seen. It smelled like tortillas and there was a bowl filled with cooked oatmeal the old woman liked to eat. Lupe closed the door and looked toward the clapboard outhouse. She knew there was no one there, but she went and looked in anyway. Then she came back and sat on an orange crate under the ramada. She felt calmer now and thought perhaps she had imagined what she heard, but she knew she was not one who imagined such things.

"Señora Quiroz, estas aqui?" she stood and called once more. As if in answer, she heard the sound of metal clanging against metal again and tried to tell where it came from. She walked slowly past the outhouse, down the steep side of a hill toward the old citrus orchard that grew on the lower slope. The trees, old and crippled, bent in strange forms toward the ground, their leaves sparse and wrinkled. There, along the thistle-covered but still evident rows between the trees, she saw what was making the noise. Cans, Folgers coffee cans—the cans Señora Quiroz kept her provisions in—and the contents themselves, scattered nearby. Pinto beans lay piled on a pillow of flour. The aroma of coffee rose to her head, black grains mixed up with white grains of arroz. The empty cans moved and shifted, rolling back and forth against each other. The metallic sounds were not as loud as before, and they were sweeter than those she had first heard, as though now that she was there they didn't have to shout for her anymore. They became like musical notes, strung haphazardly together by the wind. "Tinkle, tinkle, rrrr," the cans said, scraping gently against each other.

Lupe Reyes' eyes and feet followed the sweet voices of the rolling cans down through the rows of trees, noting scattered bunches of dried peas, lentils, and finally, the remains of gorditas already partially eaten by packrats or other small animals, until at last she found what she was looking for.

The Mexican policeman at the diner at La Cinquenta was sucking nachos and cleaning his fingernails with a toothpick when una señora de años, pero bien hecha, appeared beside him.

"Huh!" he grunted, quickly establishing his authority.

"Señor policia, I must talk to you," said Lupe Reyes, not at all timidly. She was already moving through the swinging door, and he had to follow, resentful and bored. After she told him what she had to say, he made her stand outside, waiting, until another car arrived with more police and a plainclothes detective.

In the orchard, the same grunting policeman nosed around the piles of rice and coffee like a javalina pawing the ground in search of roots, until the plainclothes detective nodded him off with a curt gesture. The detective, a clean-shaven mixed-blood wearing Levi's and a silver concho belt, went with Lupe Reyes to her house and sat down and talked to her.

"There are those who prey upon women living alone," he said. "Señora Albura, right on the corner of La Cinquenta-tres, brutally assaulted and robbed; the old woman, a white woman, who lived in a small trailer by the fork, golpiada, almost killed; and Cristina Gaspacho from the barrio, attacked while walking home with her groceries, her fingers cut off with a knife because she would not release her bag." Lupe Reyes listened to all this respectfully, even when he said, "You mujeres are easy to damage. That's just how it is. Is there no place I can take you?" His face closed down again, becoming impersonal, when she declined. "At least put a lock on your door," he threw back in parting.

Lupe Reyes sat looking at her jacal after he had gone. The door didn't fit the opening; cracks showed around it. The door itself was nothing, but hidden by the lintel was a frame of steel— the doubtful gift of a possessive and paranoid man who thought once that he could lock Lupe Reyes in her own house. Her mind went to the windows next. There was no glass in two of them—

she had nailed a torn piece of screen across them, only to keep the flies out. The other two windows wouldn't go up or down, jammed about three inches from the bottom. She welcomed the breeze that entered through them on hot nights. She thought about all these things, but they were just thoughts passing through. The rest of her mind was deep in her soul, curled up around the picture of her friend: her head twisted at an impossible angle, su bulto stretched out and covered with dry citrus leaves, as if the tree had shaken with her agony and scattered its leaves to cover her nakedness, and the blood. All the paths to Lupe Reyes' heart had been closed. If there was a miracle coming, it would never be able to arrive. She could no longer receive it, she knew now, and this hurt her as much as the rest.

All that afternoon she sat unmoving by the paloverde tree in front of the jacal. She could not have said where she went, but it was a path strewn with thorns and her feet were bare. When finally she reached deliverance from this anguish of the soul, the sun had left, but the sky still burned and the mountains were becoming huge with the mystery of darkness. She made her preparations with the door. Then Lupe Reyes lit a candle—her last one—and set it on a box near the door. Next she moved the rocks, one by one, until the ground in front of the entrance to the house was only dirt. She dug at it with her fingers until she uncovered an iron box that had once been painted yellow but now was rusted and encrusted with chunks of hardened earth. She pulled the box away from its hole, a little at a time because it was very heavy, and then took the rosary that was around her neck, kissed the crucifix, inserted it head first into the lock. The lock turned as smooth as oil.

Even before Lupe Reyes finished with everything she had
to do, night came on with a rush, stars licking the tops of trees,
seeping to the ground in liquid light. Lupe was there, waiting in
the darkness, but only the wild animals knew it, accepting her as
they did the presence of rocks or the bodies of cactus. The waning
moon had risen and sunk quickly behind the hills before an aged
coyote with withered flanks and patchy fur came up the trail
from the arroyo, sniffing the air for something to eat. He sniffed
the strange smells and, identifying them, slunk away without a
sound, like a silken shadow. And Lupe Reyes waited. She waited
that night and the next and the next. On the third night she felt
him and smelled him long before he was even close. He came
forward, drifting out of a curtain of morning glory vines at the
eastern edge of the ravine. He moved toward the jacal, unaware
that he was being drawn to it like a magnet draws a poisoned nail
from a bleeding wound. Lupe Reyes was pulling him in step by
step, winding him around his own mistakes, his mind vacant, his
lips pulling away from small sharp teeth like those of a rat. He
raised the knife in his hand as the other hand reached out and
touched the door. Then he froze in place as he listened, licking his
lips. She even heard him swallow twice against a dry throat as he
gently, so slowly, almost imperceptibly, opened the door. With a
swift motion he was inside, the door shutting behind him. Lupe
Reyes leaped up from her hiding place, dropping the iron bars
into place across the door. With an extension of the same
springing motion, she put match to kerosene, running as lightly
as a deer around the jacal, creating fire as she ran. Within seconds
the dry wood was blazing like tinder. It took only seconds for him
to identify the sounds of the crackling flames for what they were.

She heard the breaking glass, the scream of rage as he realized he could not fit through the windows, and the mighty kicking and shattering of the door, the snarling of a wild beast as he tore the wood from its hinges and pressed forward, but was prevented by the iron bars and the flames already rising to the height of a man. He tried to grasp and shake them but the heat cast him back. He never heard the gunfire that shattered his mind, ending the fear one second before everything was consumed in flames.

She sat through the night keeping vigil, the instrument of her mercy, a Colt .45 with a shining silver stock, held in her hands. The silver was engraved with a beautiful woman's face, half in light, half in shadow, and the metal was warm and loving from the heat of her hands.

The sun had risen long ago, and the little sparrows had returned to play in the nearby trees, before the ashes had cooled enough to walk on. She gathered the knife and the charred bones that were left, carried them to the citrus orchard and buried them on the spot where Carmelita Quiroz had fallen. When she returned, she remembered her tapalo. But when she took it from the paloverde tree she saw that the center of the black square was bleached white as if by an intense light. And for a moment, beneath the moving shadows of the tree, Lupe Reyes saw her own face among the threads.

Come Rain or Come Shine

Venian los vientos como rabia queriendo hechar abajo el jacal, the winds came rabid, intent on pulling down the shack that already hung like a stack of matchsticks at the edge of the river. It wasn't warm anywhere, but the bus stop where Trudi waited was the worst.

She leaned back on her stiletto heels and scratched a match to life with one fingernail. It flared for an instant of pretend warmth and lit up her face like a red coal before the wind sucked it out again. Pulling her thin coat tighter, Trudi allowed her teeth to chatter; it made her feel less cold. At last she saw the 8:10 Greyhound to Phoenix rounding the curve at Three Corners. A wall of dust came tearing across the desert and slammed into the bus. Showers of dirt spread around the wheels as the door swung open and Trudi, battling the wind, tottered up the steps.

Outside the jacal where Trudi had walked from earlier, the wind rose to a shriek and crashed into the house. The windows shook, threatening to break. The door broke open and struck the wall. Mecha was up in an instant, jamming a chair under the knob and crossing herself.

"Ay! Que viento tan bravo!" she said. "The wind would like to blow us away."

"Que me saque a mi," said Poncha. She sat on a chair by the bed, wrapped in a black rebozo, her feet barely peeking out from under her long black skirt. "Let it take me and see what it gets!" She smacked her gums.

"You're a piece of gold, Abuelita," Chuchee said to Poncha. She managed to stand up on her uneven legs and flail an arm—it was impossible to say where it was intended to point—in the air. The first words she said always made sense. But then she added the second line, like she always did, shouting, "Tlamohuanchan! Tlalocan, Tlalocan!" bouncing up and down on the bed.

"Si, mi hita, si," said Poncha soothingly, and took the bundle of jerking limbs, the almost weightless body, in her arms. Murmuring, she stroked the child's curly head and wet back and arms and chest with her solid, reassuring grandmother's hands that alone could quiet Chuchee, quell her anxiety that Abuelita might go away and never come back. She jerked and trembled and slept, her open mouth drooling on the pañuelo Poncha kept folded beneath her chin.

Chuchee's mother, Mecha, forced the wadded newspapers in the cracks around the door, quenching the drafts, and returned to her chair by the stove. She pushed her greying hair back into its bun with hairpins and then looked in the cradle, fussed with the blanket, wiggled her fingers in front of her son's eyes, always looking for any change in his blank stare. She patted his chest and sighed. She began to hum a song. In the small circle of warmth by the stove, she hummed and Poncha crooned, both women making wordless comforting sounds that softened the voice of the howling wind.

The bus on its way to Phoenix had originated across the border in Dos Piedras and was full of Mexicans returning to the cotton fields in the Valley of the Sun. The interior of the bus was steeped in their smells. Their cloth shopping bags were stuffed full of calavasitas, corn tortillas and cafe wrapped in paper, and sometimes a mango or two that had been concealed from the border officials inside their undershirts. One of them had his change of clothes wrapped around an effigy of La Guadalupe. Fearful of going anywhere without her, they carried her back and forth across the border, praying for the health of their families on their way there and praying for more work on the way back, touching her bulto frequently to still their fear. In low urgent tones they talked to each other all the way, sometimes erupting in strident laughter.

Trudi could barely stand the resignation all around her. She hated the whole idea of their acceptance, saw it as the weight that kept them in their place. Because she felt this acceptance was inextricable from the God of La Raza, she was angry at that God too. It was true, there was nothing they could do about

Miguelito's blindness, nothing they could do about Chuchee's crippled body or Poncha's heart condition. The children had been born that way and Poncha was old and could not live forever. "I have to die from something," she was fond of saying, to get everyone used to the idea. No, it had to go back to before they got that way, Trudi decided, something they were doing wrong as a race, that brought this endless stream of daños upon them, as though they had asked for it. And were still asking for it, wanting to be slaves to suffering, poverty, illness and death, because they thought it was demanded by their God, and piety should be their only reward in this life.

As usual, these thoughts scrambled her emotions and Trudi felt a familiar desperation rising inside. She had been a fool to think there was any getting out of the life she had. How could she? Taking classes at the junior college had been a fantasy, one she couldn't even let Mecha and Poncha know about. Easier not to see the pain of her inevitable disappointment in their eyes. Chicana pride was for those who could afford it.

As the busload of Mexicans plowed through the desert Trudi looked out at the endless wastes of rock and cactus. She tried not to think about what lay at the other end. She carried her gift, a handful of aguacates wrapped in a pañuelo, on her lap so they wouldn't get smashed. Big difference it will make to him, she thought. Also, she didn't want to be smelling like fruit when she saw the doctor. Her hair had been carefully sprinkled with rose water and she had carefully dusted her breasts with polvos de rosa. Her stockings were without runs, her dress freshly washed and ironed.

The bus let her off at a major intersection. She walked from there, block after block of iron fence, barbed wire stretching across the top. Nicely clipped green lawns faded back to a row of identical white buildings, except that some had bars in the windows. There was no one else walking. Cars whizzed by, sheltered from the wind and dust by speed and tightly closed windows. Trudi walked as quickly as she could in her high heels, her head down, a scarf tied around her hair to keep it in place. She walked through the main gate down the long sidewalk to the Administration Building of the State Hospital and went in.

A few minutes later she came out and walked around the building to the back where the canteen was. She saw him immediately, sitting on a bench, looking at the ground.

"Hola, Papa," she said.

"Oh hi, Trudi," he said in English without expression on his face. His head was shaved, his mustache gone. His beautiful wavy black hair was gone; he had become old. Trudi opened the pañuelo to show him the aguacates.

"Oh hey, you brought me some aguacates," he said, but made no attempt to take them. Trudi handed them to him one at a time and he put each one in his mouth whole, chewing noisily, swallowing the large lump at once and spitting the pit out on the ground. He ate the five aguacates and then asked, "Did you bring me any more aguacates, Trudi?"

"No, that's all," she said.

"Okay." He was shivering.

"Don't you have a coat?" asked Trudi. But he didn't look at her or answer. "Why don't we go inside where it's warm?"

"No, I have to stay out here," he said.

"Come on, Ed," said a voice. An attendant in a white jacket and pants, white shoes and socks had come up behind them. "Time to go in," he said cheerfully, nodding at Trudi.

"Okay," said Eduardo. He stood up.

"Adios, Papi," said Trudi. "Luego te veo. I'll come back as soon as I can." But he didn't turn around, just walked away shivering, his hands in his pockets, the attendant following.

Trudi remained sitting on the bench, the pañuelo still open on her knees, looking at the pile of wet aguacate pits by her feet. She remembered the squishing noise as each one emerged from her father's lips. The physical sensation of this memory made her feel like throwing up. She swallowed, folded the pañuelo quickly and put it in her pocket.

When she reached the doctor's door the scarf was off her head, her coat was on her arm revealing a brown dress with purple flowers, and she was smiling. He motioned her in, looked hurriedly down the empty corridor, and locked the door. She sensed the movement of his body come up behind her as she stood at the window. The hand he placed on her shoulder was not pleasant or unpleasant, just heavy. A pack of old newspapers might have felt the same way. From the second floor, Trudi watched big American cars at the entrance passing by fat palm trees that were flapping and tortured by the wind. The strangeness of the outside world made his caresses more stark, as if her breasts were brass balls and his hands those of a merchant searching for defects. There were none.

"Oh my sweet, my sweet," he said. That was how she knew when it was the end and she could put down her dress and go into the bathroom. When she came out, he handed her a paper bag and said nothing. She didn't thank him. He opened the door, looked quickly down the corridor, and closed the door after her. She wondered if he was watching as she walked down the sidewalk and along the high barbed-wire fence, past the buildings with bars on the windows...but she thought he probably wasn't. Just as he hadn't smelled the rose water on her hair or seen her legs in high heels. Only if these things weren't there would he have noticed.

Trudi didn't open the bag until she got off the bus at Three Corners. She fished out a ten dollar bill, closed the sack again and went into the tavern. She ordered some antojitos but nothing to drink, then changed her mind and drank a tequila straight. When the antojitos came she didn't feel like eating. She wrapped them in a napkin and put them in the paper sack. She sat around a while longer, but no one else came in and the jukebox was silent. The waitress-bartender was in back talking to the dishwasher, so she picked up her change and went to the market next door. She bought some dried pescado, some panocha, ten pounds of beans, a sack of flour, some lard, a gallon of milk and a box of animal crackers. The hamburger didn't look so good so she got the ribs, enough for everybody. She threw in a small bottle of apricot brandy.

She was struggling up the trail to the jacal with the heavy bags when Mecha came hurrying toward her and took one of the sacks from her arms.

"Ay, que bueno, ya venistes," she said. "I'm glad you're back. Como te fue—no trabajastes muy duro? How was work?" Trudi muttered something incomprehensible but Mecha wasn't listening. She went on talking, excited because of the groceries. She put the bag on the table and immediately went over and put some sticks in the stove to get it hot for the tortillas. Poncha was asleep on the bed with Chuchee, and Trudi tiptoed around them to get to the cradle. Miguelito's blind eyes were crossed as he tried to suck his thumb and pull on his toes at the same time. He was always so quiet.

"I got the medicine for Chuchee and the vitamins and the pills for Nana," whispered Trudi.

"Dios te lo page, mi hita, por todo tu trabajo," said Mecha. The gratitude in her voice made Trudi sad. She didn't tell her mother what she thought of God's rewards.

They made the tortillas together, and when the third one was cooking Chuchee sat up in bed and said, "I smell gorditas!" Then she said, "Tlamohuanchan! Tlalocan! Tlalocan!" bouncing up and down on her knees. The bouncing woke up Poncha, who got up, wrapping her ragged rebozo around her shoulders, and went to the groceries on the table.

She picked up the bottle of apricot brandy without a word and put it in the big pocket of her skirt. Then she got a clean dry diaper from the rope strung behind the stove and started changing Miguelito. She took the dirty diaper outside and scrubbed it in the bandeja with a bar of Lava soap. She threw the dirty water in the yard, brought the clean diaper back in and hung it behind the stove.

"God, Nana, your hands are like ice," said Trudi, rubbing the old woman's hands between her own.

"Quita, you're going to get the tortillas dirty," said Poncha, but she was pleased with the attention.

They ate with the urgency of long denial, hungrily savoring each bite as though it could be ripped from their mouths at any second. But Trudi could not forget where the food came from. It was with a touch of irony that she stripped the meat from the ribs, ate the rolled tortilla, put a lump of panocha in her cafe and tasted the thick black sweetness.

But it was irony without regret. She couldn't remake, with a wave of her hand, this collection of junk that was their jacal, nor remove the afflictions that were their everyday existence. But the ones she loved were eating and that was worth whatever she did, to see their happiness and enjoyment. All the poor had anyway, she thought, were these moments, tasting the sweetness of panocha in the coffee, going to bed with a full stomach. And all this family had was her.

It was Poncha who fed Chuchee. Chuchee wouldn't accept food from anyone else. She took the partially chewed morsel of meat from her grandmother's fingers with her mouth, making a hum like a bumblebee as she ate. Feeding Miguelito his bottle, Trudi looked lovingly at his curly black hair, his small perfectly shaped mouth, his tiny fingers that gripped her own with such determination. Only his blind eyes moved this way and that, without intent, and she was glad when he closed them and slept.

That night Trudi stared at the room. The small pile of books she never opened anymore were scattered by her bed. Across the room Poncha was snoring, Chuchee humming, Mecha shifting now and then from her spot beside them, her arm hanging protectively over the cradle. That was the hardest for Trudi, hearing them, not being able to stop hearing them, near her in the same room, the sound of their living. Her awareness of how fragile it all was, dependent on the fever and attractiveness of her body and her willingness to use it that way.

She thought of Doctor Melchner; he kept his agreement. The medicines and the money were always given without question or comment. She did her part and he did his. That was all there was to it. She couldn't ask for better. She searched her emotions but she felt nothing, except to wonder how long it could last.

Trudi got up quietly, put on jeans and a sweater and tennies, put a few dollars in her pocket and took her coat from the hook by the door. She stood by the jacal for a few moments, getting accustomed to the darkness and the way the mesquites moved with the wind.

Only at night did she feel no animosity toward the desert— at night when everything was obscured and smooth with darkness. In daylight she saw only the cruelty, the terrible heat or the terrible cold, the nothingness of brush and rock without water, without oasis. At those times she said the words, I gotta get out of here, I gotta get out of here, like a litany—not to God but to that tiny thing inside of her that still hoped somewhere there was something else. But now in the darkness, walking, breathing, she was alive, alive with each footstep.

She heard the jukebox at Three Corners before she saw the light. Jesse's playing his old 78s again, she thought. It must be dead in there tonight. The violins and sax came and went on the wind, and then turned into words, I'm gonna love you like nobody's loved you... Days may be cloudy or sunny; we're in or we're out of the money. I'm gonna love you...

What kind of world did those people live in? Trudi thought as the record ended. She came out of the desert and crossed the road to the tavern. There were no cars coming or going either way, just the road vanishing into darkness. The wind jerked the door out of her hand, and it bounced against the wall.

"Sorry," she called. Jesse shrugged his shoulders. He was leaning on the bar fiddling with the knobs on the TV.

"Damn wind's screwing up the antenna again," he said.

"Where's Earla?" asked Trudi, sitting down.

"I sent her home early."

"Another hot night in the ol' corral?"

"The weekend it ain't," said Jesse, "but hey, it's better than staying at home." He had a picture but no sound. "So who needs sound?" he said. Trudi looked.

"Got the old Vegas channel, huh?"

"A man's gotta have his entertainment." Trudi looked at the images for a minute. "If they were really lesbians, I could dig it," she said.

"Looks real to me," said Jesse. "Okay, okay, but who cares if it's real?"

"It feels wrong," said Trudi. She meant it.

"How's the Doc?" asked Jesse. He turned off the TV and got a couple of frosted glasses from the fridge.

"Quick and easy. That's how I like 'em," said Trudi. She laughed. Jesse didn't.

"You need a real guy in your life," he said. "Somebody who cares about you." He put crushed ice in the blender, added tequila and lime and mixed it up. Trudi waited till the noise stopped.

"It's better this way. He knows what he's getting and I know what I'm giving. No mistakes. Everybody's happy." Jesse poured the drinks, shaking his head.

"Listen," said Trudi, "whoever gets me gets my family. What guy wants that?"

"I said it before," said Jesse. "Come and work here..."

"You know why I can't. We'd see too much of each other and you know what would happen."

He leaned toward her. "I can pay for it just like he can, baby."

"Stop it!" She slammed her drink down, spilling some out.

Jesse started wiping around the glass, not looking at her. "Yeah, I know I'm off base, but it's just that...well, you know how I feel."

"Yeah, you want to fuck me, Jesse—so what? I'm one man's whore. I'm not going to be another man's mistress."

Jesse nodded, red-faced. He filled her glass from the blender again. They drank.

"Listen," said Trudi, "if you weren't here, I don't know what I'd do sometimes, okay? Can't we just leave it at that?"

He nodded again. "Yeah." Sighed. "Okay, it's just I wish you'd just give in to it, baby. I mean, it would be easier if you weren't so darn beautiful..."

Trudi put her glass down.

"See what I mean? God, I'm sick of this shit. Every time we're alone. Can't you forget your cock for one night? I'm tired. Tired!" Trudi stood up too fast. For a moment she was afraid she was going to fall down. She held onto the edge of the bar. "I can only sell myself so many ways, don't you get it?"

Insulted, and then contrite, Jesse admitted, "I didn't mean—look, I'm sorry. I really am. I'd like to help you out, that's all."

"Sure." Trudi drank the rest of the tequila sour, put the glass back down on the bar and said so long. Outside, the stars seemed to be moving further away from the earth. Walking away in the thickening darkness, she heard the stereo again. *I'm gonna love you like nobody's loved you come rain or come shine...*

She was glad when she couldn't hear it anymore.

The jacal was the way she had left it. Except Chuchee had stopped humming and was now making a kind of lisping sound as her breath went in and out, her bad arm twitching on Poncha's shoulder. Trudi looked in the cradle. Miguelito was awake, sucking his fingers. She felt his diaper but it was dry. "Hey you, watcha doing, huh?" In the dark his open eyes did not seem blind; they looked back at her in wide-eyed contemplation. She let him play with her fingers and then went to bed herself.

But she couldn't sleep. Finally she opened her eyes and, staring at the wall for a minute, realized the pattern she saw on the wall was from the light coming through the curtain. It was dawn. Then she heard the sound of an engine. It cut in and out and then stayed, gradually coming closer. Trudi put on her jeans and sweater and opened the door enough to see out toward the direction of the noise: a Highway Patrol 4x4 had come off road and stopped at the bunch of saguaros at the bottom of the trail. Trudi closed the door behind herself quietly and went down to meet the cop who had climbed out and was looking up at the house. One hand on his hip, he said, "This the Ochoa place?"

"Yes," said Trudi.

"You the daughter?"

"Yeah, what's the matter?"

"I got some bad news, Miss—is your mother at home?"

"Better tell me. She doesn't speak English very well."

"Your father, Eduardo? Well, he's been in an accident."

"How could he? He's in the hospital."

"He apparently left the hospital grounds last evening without authorization and jumped a freight to the Pueblo. He fell trying to get off, and well, you better come with me now."

"How bad?" asked Trudi. Her throat was dry and she could barely get the words out.

The patrolman shrugged. "You all better come if you want to see him," he repeated.

"Can you wait a minute?" Trudi ran up the trail. She saw Mecha's face peering through the window.

"Tu papa?" she asked and covered her mouth with her hand.

Trudi nodded. "Dice que nos apuremos. He said we should go now."

Poncha, awake and sitting up in bed, said, "Me quedo yo. I'll stay with the children." Her voice was shaking and frightened.

"No, why don't you and Poncha take Miguelito, Ma, and I'll stay with Chuchee?" Trudi said.

"Que asemos?" Mecha, eyes filled with tears, looked at Poncha, then at Trudi. "Te necesito para hablar. We need your English." She was trying to put on a dress with fumbling fingers.

"Yeah, I forgot."

"De todos modos, Chuchee would be afraid if I wasn't here," said Poncha, heavily. "Hay, tu ve por mi hijo," she pleaded to Mecha. "Look after my son." She pulled her tapalo down over her eyes and sat holding her rosary, her fingers moving fitfully over the beads.

"Horita venimos," Trudi told Poncha, squeezing her hand. It was like ice. The old woman only nodded, her cheeks wet.

Trudi grabbed her coat, made sure she had some money and led her mother down to the waiting Highway Patrol car. The two women sat in back, and Trudi told Mecha what happened.

"Yo se que nos venia a ver, he was coming to see us, I know it," Mecha whispered. She was ashamed for the cop to hear her speaking Spanish.

When they got to Community Hospital Mecha was trembling so badly, Trudi told her to wait in the lobby—she would go first and see how it was. The cop greeted the nurses at the station cheerfully and one of them, a heavyset woman, called out to another, "Hey, two-eleven out of ICU?"

"Yeah, he's out," the other said.

Consulting her clipboard, the first nurse said, "The doctor wants to talk to you. Wait a moment. I'll page him."

After the doctor said what he had to say, Trudi went and got Mecha. She was sitting on a big green armchair, folding and unfolding her pañuelo. For the next few minutes Trudi suspended time inside of herself. It's not going to happen. It's too late. It's too late, she said to herself over and over again.

As soon as they saw him Mecha grabbed Trudi's arm, and bracing themselves, they walked the rest of the way to the bed. At first he seemed not to be breathing, but then they saw the rise and fall of his chest.

"Ya le quitaron todo?" said Mecha softly accepting. "They took everything away." She was referring to the life support. Trudi nodded. She couldn't speak.

Mother and daughter waited, afraid to take their eyes away even for an instant. Then his face stretched and his tongue came out—he was trying to speak. He was saying something, and Mecha said, "Ay, tu, mi hita, haber que dice—habla en ingles. What does he say?" Trudi bent down. He didn't move or open his eyes. She was going to straighten up again when she heard him say, pushing out the words one by one, and then in a rush,

"Now...you...can...tell...Doctor...Melchner...togotohell." And then he said "Tlalocan" softly, and nothing more. After a shocked moment, Trudi said to herself so only she could hear, "Oh, you fool, Papa. You fool."

She shook her head, bent near him again and whispered, "Gracias, Papa, gracias."

Glossary: Aztec, Nahuatl.

Tlamohuanchan   a mythical place of origin, Eden.

Tlalocan   the place of *Tlaloc*, the Mexican god of rain, who presides over *Tlalocan*, a luxurious paradise for those who die in Tlaloc's favor.

El Velatorio de Chapa Diaz

The Angel let herself in through the back door. Her wings were so big she had to fold them over, shaking them out again on the other side. Her feathers rustling in sequential rows was like the startling rush of a flock of birds, a rippling staccato.

"Why didn't you just come through the wall?" asked Chapa, a little irritated. "If I could do that, I'd never walk with my feet," she said from the bed.

The Angel preened her feathers like a graceful swan. "I'd have to disintegrate and reassemble and it's a lousy sensation."

"Oh." Chapa looked through the window. Outside, the eucalyptus trees on the Central Coast were struggling under a late spring, their leaves swollen with rainwater and hanging like ripe bananas. Big round clouds seemed to snag in the treetops and fall between the branches. But that's not what Chapa saw. What she saw was the desert, vast and dry, stretching to the mountains. She saw a fair sky rising endlessly above them, painted with purple clouds among the peaks.

"Why were you so depressed?" asked the Angel.

Chapa started at the voice. She had already forgotten. "Oh, ya ves...about being sick...and dying." She imagined she saw the plastic tubes snaking over and around her, wrapping her up in their coils. Chapa's brown eyes were deep wells. "Doing things wrong over and over again gets boring. Don't we ever get someplace where we can stay?" The Angel sitting on her haunches stopped crouching at the foot of the bed, got up and came closer. Her skin was wet and shining copper. The tips of her feathers became a translucent burning.

"Ya te dije," said Chapa, in the most stubborn voice she could summon. "Don't try to take me cause I'm not going yet!" The fire on the Angel's wings went away. "Anyway, how come you don't have a black dress and a machete?"

The Angel grinned, "What you see is what you get."

"Don't try to trick me or anything," said Chapa.

The Angel cleared her throat and said conversaionally, "When I came across the border, they were holding a poor cholo and his wife for dos limones she had hidden in her dress."

"Mama used to hide the limones in a towel," said Chapa. "She gave them to us to suck on the train so we wouldn't get sick. But we always threw up anyway—on the towel. Then all the limones were safe." Chapa was breathing heavily with the memory. "Cuando era chiquita, the basca would come all at one time. And then I forgot about it right away."

"I think you've said something very profound," said the Angel. She looked innocent, but interested.

"Yeah, yeah," said Chapa, "no mas, I don't want dying to be like I was swallowing a tablespoon of castor oil, you know?"

The Angel pulled her wings in like a tent, showing a new face, full of challenge. "Tell me."

Chapa swallowed. She saw the clouds moving out from the mountains to cover the sun. She was sad but she wanted to talk about it.

"Ay, in life there isn't a harder thing than when love goes. Se queda uno con todo ese amor, and somehow you have to tear it out of your heart. Que dolor! Every time, trying to do that con estilo, with taste, was the hardest thing."

The Angel nodded.

"Where does love go when the flame doesn't burn anymore? Where does that querencia go?" The Angel didn't answer. "Well then," demanded Chapa, "why did so much have to end? How did it happen that I could not save one pair of arms, one heart that loved me for real? Tell me that!"

The Angel was silent.

Chapa was angry. "Why don't you explain me these things?"

"None of my speeches seem appropriate right now," said the Angel.

"Of all the Angels, how come I have to get one that's not even Mexican? You talk like you go to the University but you can't tell me anything?"

"We brushed wings plenty of times. We even brushed souls," the Angel said quietly.

But Chapa said, "Callate! How would you know, you, dressed up in light!" The words hung in the air and fell.

The Angel said, "The best you felt—that was me."

"No! The best you ever feel—that's me!" cried Chapa. This was one thing she knew for sure.

The door closed with a soft clunk. "Mama's talking to herself again," said Roberto to Rosie, coming back into the kitchen. He knew he should sit down to eat but he was too restless.

"What's she saying?" asked five-year-old Jesus. "Is she talking about me?" He grinned up at his teenaged sister and brother, then with his fork stabbed at the empty plate Rosie put in front of him.

"I don't think she knows what she's talking about," Rosie kneeled to put her arms around Jesus and give him a hug. She finished putting out the plates and forks, and Roberto got three glasses to fill with water. He leaned over the sink and looked through the tiny window at the trees behind the trailer. They had been there seven months and he hated the trailer park more every day.

Since the apples they'd picked in the fall there had been little work all winter and now, when it was supposed to be spring, the rain kept falling, day after day after day. If it didn't stop soon all the strawberries would rot in the fields and there wouldn't be any work for anybody. Roberto pushed his hair away from his eyes—he needed a haircut bad—and said angrily, "I wish we'd never come to this pinche cold place."

The sun came out from the clouds for a minute and the sky was deep blue. Soon it would be dark. The sound of the cars on the freeway was a constant whine of high gears. Later, at night when there weren't so many cars, they would be able to hear the waves breaking on the beach. The blue sky lingered for a final second of fluid clarity, and the clouds came in swiftly like thick fog. The sun was extinguished and everything was grey again. The euca- lyptus trees stood dense and heavy, a solid mass of forbidding forest.

His anger turned sad and quiet. Roberto said, "We shoulda never left the desert."

"Yeah, and done what?" snapped Rosie. "There wasn't any work there." She was tired of hearing Roberto say the same thing a hundred times. She was the one who had to make the food stamps stretch to the end of each month. It had been her idea to go to the beach, especially on the weekends when the weather was good, and get the Coke and beer cans before the rangers got there in the evenings.

She softened, remembering how Roberto had made a game out of it for Jesus so he'd forget about being cold and cranky. But then Roberto had run off without a word, his face red with shame, when he saw some girls watching him go through the trash. Rosie had gritted her teeth and kept right on hauling out the aluminum cans, putting them in the shopping bag.

"So what kind of work we got here?" Roberto asked. "Pinche fields drowning in water," he said with disgust. He sighed, setting the glasses filled with water on the table, and sat down to eat the tamales Rosie had made. He cut up his tamale savagely with his fork, thinking, If Mama hadn't gotten sick...But he didn't want to think about that. It would be warm in the desert already, and this year he would have been on the varsity team, and graduating, and maybe...

Jesus had stopped eating, pieces of meat and leftover masa still on his plate. He was tearing at a tamale leaf, shredding long greasy pieces of it and piling them on the table. Rosie slapped her little brother lightly on the top of his head. "Stop making more work for me."

Jesus started crying. "I want Mama to be here."

Roberto got up from his chair and picked up Jesus. "Me too," he said, to comfort the boy. "Me too."

Rosie looked up at Roberto. "Let's not argue anymore, okay?"

"Okay." Roberto was happy to forget about it. He swung Jesus in the air and around in a circle, then dangled him upside down. Jesus squealed with laughter.

"You're going to make him throw up," Rosie warned, but she was smiling too.

"I won't throw up, Roberto! Do it some more!" shouted Jesus.

"Naw, not till after you finish eating," said Roberto, depositing Jesus back in his chair. The boy obediently picked up a morsel of masa and put it in his mouth to chew.

Chapa saw all of them through the lenses of her heart, heard them speaking as though they were right there, eating tamales and arguing in the hospital corridor. No, I'm not in the hospital. I'm at home, she thought, looking around, touching her wrists, her face, for the ever-present tubes. But nothing was there. Yes, gracias a Dios, I'm at home.

But where is home? Confused, unsure, she raised her head to look over the windowsill. The desert sky was still the translucent blue of a spring afternoon. The clouds weren't there now, and the mountains were closer. She thought if she could reach out a hand, she could touch them. But her arms were too heavy to lift.

The Angel said, "What else are you sure about, Chapa?" She was patient and infinitely kind.

Chapa decided to spit it out. "Quise ser buena, the way I was when I was a child. But living took the good all away. Now I'm like a spool with all the thread unwound. Me pesa, y no veo mas que la oscuridad. It's so dark and the things I regret make me afraid." This last was the hardest to say, but after she said it she just wanted to sleep.

The Angel persisted. "Which one did you love most?"

Chapa didn't have to think about it, and the Angel's wings quivered slightly when Chapa said, "The father of Rosa. Tan maravilloso! Like a black panther stalking me. He had my heart in his mouth, sabes? O si, he was careful not to pierce it, but all the same, a few drops of my blood came out from between his teeth." Her tears had dried long ago, but uncovering the place that never seemed to fill in her heart made her so weak she could barely speak.

"He was the one who stole my soul. He is the one I will not name." She tried to sit up. "Listen...do you hear the hawk crying far above the cactus? Her children's hunger drives her like a knife!" This was the extent of her strength and she fell back. The Angel was listening, her cheek resting against one wing, her lips just open, her breath barely moving.

Chapa wrestled suddenly inside her flesh, and though she could not raise her head, she spoke more strongly, more gaily, teeth shining, because this memory was full of the Mexican sun.

"And there was Miguel. He wore feathers in his hat like an indio. He was the son of Tenochtitlan; a parrot with red and blue feathers sat on his shoulder, cooing like a dove when we kissed."

"And how about Roberto's father? Who was he?"

"Ah, Roberto's father! Efraim. I was so young—I was afraid even of his soft hands and careful way. When at last I came to him, he knew my weakness. I crawled to him on a blanket which he covered with jewels. I picked them up one by one and put them here, against my breasts. What breasts, hermosas, I had then, and the jewels—rubies and emeralds, sapphires and pearls—the colors of blood-red wine and the eyes of tigers shining from the jungle. Stones pale and soft like the face of the moon. It could not last, of course. They came and took him away to a prison where the other men, the animals, made short work of his tender flesh." She gasped with the memory, and then Efraim's face flew away from her. Chapa's voice was flat, "He was dead before his child...before Roberto took his first breath." She paused to breathe. "They are gone. They are all gone now." Her face was lax, empty, her eyes staring.

The Angel was suffering. When Chapa looked up and saw it, her eyes grew bright and fierce. Bitter anger colored her voice, raspy with emotion.

"Ya veo que sabes lo que es vivir y sufrir, pero ya ves, no se me olvidan esos momentos, esas flores de esperanza, mis hijos, la unica felicidad."[1] She raised her voice in terror of what she was going to say next. "De donde vienes tu, alli ire, pero con amargura me paro en frente de Dios."[2]

The Angel trembled, her light pale. Then her light began to glisten wetly, her innocence damaged like nectar spilled from a rose.

Chapa shouted, "No, nunca ire perdonarle a Dios el infierno de este mundo!"[3] Her wailing fell to silence and she refused to see the Angel anymore. The darkness that settled around her was the blackest thing she'd ever seen.

"Do you hear it?" asked Rosie.

"What?" said Roberto. Jesus had gone to sleep in his lap and he continued to stroke the child, the way Chapa had stroked him, loving and gentle strokings of the head. So he, himself, was soothed and calm when Rosie's answer came.

"El Angel de la Muerte—no deja en paz la casa."

"Come on, Rosie, don't give me that regressive india shit." But Roberto's hand trembled.

"Why not?" asked Rosie, shivering in such a way that Roberto regretted his outburst. "I am also my father's daughter, Roberto, and there *are* ghosts—our mother's ghosts—and they won't go till they get what they came for." She said it with such conviction, that Roberto could only stare at her, wordless. He finally nodded at Jesus, asleep in his arms.

In spite of the rough Levi's and man's shirt she wore, Rosie's body seemed young and fragile as she reached to take Jesus from Roberto. She carried him to the room he'd shared with Chapa these past months. His small stained fingers, smelling like tamales, curled at her breast.

When Rosie got to Chapa's door, she couldn't go in. She stood in the hallway, with Jesus' head pressed against her neck, feeling him breathing, asleep, trusting. So she took him and put him down in her own bed, bunching the pillows around him to protect him in case he rolled over in his sleep. Then she went to Chapa's room and closed the door behind her.

Her mother's face was calm; she slept without discomfort, breathing easily. God, when will this end, thought Rosie. She longed to be free to go her own way, free to live the life she was learning about. Free from sins and penance. Free from huevos rancheros and gorditas, free from carne asada y menudo. Free from the tastes and the smells of her people. Free to live in another world, to make her own identity not just accept one based on culture.

Her restlessness made her walk from one side of the room to the other, hands digging in the pockets of her jeans. "You're crazy," Roberto had said, revealing what he really felt when he wasn't trying to be tough. "How can you be something other than what you are? We *are* La Raza. We'll carry it with us until we die. You'll go away," he'd said bitterly, "and then you'll want it all back, and who of our blood will love you then?" He'd almost cried but ran out instead, slamming the door. He hadn't come back to eat, but had crept into the dark house and gone to bed without a word. The next day he looked like he always did, unmoved, unbothered. They never spoke about it again.

Rosie stopped pacing and sat down next to Chapa. Looking at her mother's grey hair, at her closed eyes that she would never see open again, Rosie felt memories flood her whole being, pressing painfully against her mind and heart. God, why did Mama have to go? Why couldn't she have stayed until they could make things better? To see her and Roberto and Jesus...?

Rosie's hands were tightly clenched. She wanted to break La Muerte's bones with a hammer. Her arms shook with rage and the desire to strike and strike until there was nothing left that could take Chapa away.

Rosie blinked through her tears. She could have been on the honor roll this year, and how proud Chapa would have been. She smoothed her mother's forehead but there was no sign Chapa felt anything.

"You kept telling me how intelligent I was, to get an education," Rosie whispered. She sorted through images of Chapa getting up at dawn to work in the fields, counting out the change for the bus to school, telling her to study hard. And now it was ending like this, before Chapa could see what Rosie would become. Now it was too late to ever make her understand the thing Rosie had been too angry and hurt to talk about before: Chapa had made her learn but she hadn't known—couldn't have known—that it pushed Rosie away. How could she have understood the thoughts and ideas that came between them, leaving Chapa alone, an exile in a strange country. And me too, Rosie thought, her tears coming in a gulping torrent. She could barely breathe now. *Roberto was right. I will be alone with what I know and with my memories—the same way you were, Mama.* In that instant, Rosie understood how alike they were, mother and daughter. And then a strange calm came over her. She was struck by her mother's face—by the bright, peaceful eyes filled with abiding patience. She stared into this living memory and it came to her all in one piece: Chapa, for her daughter's sake, had accepted being left behind, had known that would be the cost. But she had never stopped loving Rosie.

Rosie got up, bent over and rested her flushed cheek against Chapa's white one. She knew there was one thing she could do for both of them: she could bend her anger and her fears and make them something else. Whatever she accomplished would always be connected to Chapa. She kissed her mother's cheek, wiped her shirt sleeve across her eyes and went to find Roberto.

He was still sitting in the same chair, his brow furrowed. He looked away when he saw her, but she went up to him and touched his arm.

"Come and look at her." Rosie gently pulled him to get up. Roberto stood up reluctantly, but then he grasped Rosie's hand in a fierce grip, frightened of the feelings he had pushed away all day. He couldn't resist anymore. Somehow, he knew he needed the sorrow.

"I don't know if I can," he whispered, his eyes dark. "But I want to," and his eyes filled with tears.

The Angel had been standing in the corner for a long time, like a statue, eyes closed, shielded by her long pin feathers that reached to the floor. Her body was one slim radiating moment of loveliness, and Chapa stared and stared, at the face that was perfect beyond belief but did not invite another's touch. Chapa remembered the church calendars of long ago, with the beautiful pictures of famous paintings, the glowing colors, and she thought, I am seeing what Rafael saw, and the wonder echoed in her mind over and over again, what Rafael saw. The tears welled up and spilled down her cheeks. The Angel opened her eyes instantly, and her eyes were grey with large dark pupils that rarely blinked. The Angel stayed where she was. They watched each other across the room.

When Chapa could talk, she said, "How do you feel?"

"Are you sorry?" asked the Angel, curious.

Chapa didn't know if the Angel meant sorry for what she said to God or sorry for not offering comfort. Her refusal shocked her now, and she decided the two things were the same. But she didn't want sorry to be the last thing she said, so she added, with tenderness, "But that's the way I am," knowing it was no longer true.

The Angel's wings stretched upward to the ceiling; they looked like they would cover the walls. Chapa felt dwarfed by their size and magnificence. She felt small and withered in a large bed, smothered by the weight of the blankets. She found one desire still left: to walk in the desert again, smell the sage after a rain, and feel her brown skin warm from the sun. And never leave.

"Come with me," spoke the Angel, and as strange as it seemed to her, Chapa did. The window became a door that widened like the Angel's wings, and Chapa walked through it. She walked past the wide-leafed maguey plants in their adobe ollas, down the steps, and across the smooth blue tiles of the patio. She shaded her eyes with her hand and looked toward the mountains. They came very close, their full flanks covered with golden-thorned cholla. She saw the mountains growing out of the earth, out of spirit; more than anything, Chapa felt that desire again to be...She reached for the many beautiful flowers of the mountain and her heart poured out of her.

The Angel was no longer there.

---

[1] "I see now that you know what it is to live and suffer; but still, I don't forget those moments, those flowers of hope, my children, the only happiness."

[2] "Where you come from is where I'm going, but I face God with bitterness."

[3] "No, I won't forgive God the hell in this world!"

2 Rock Blues

I told her not to break my heart, but she did it anyway," said Ruby T to herself. She was used to talking to herself. She talked to herself more than she talked to anyone else, and she had plenty to say. It was all about that bitch, Aires, who had been stringing Ruby T around sideways and backwards until she hardly knew her own name. She didn't even want to face Ma Pache, that's how bad it was. And Ma Pache was the most important person in Ruby T's life. When it came to family, that is.

On her way to the border Ruby T stopped at the canyon, hoping there she might be able to think clearly and come to some kind of decision about Aires. She rolled her shirt sleeves up another inch, until they were stretched tight over her biceps, and ground the truck down into first gear. The creek had swollen. As she entered the canyon, water was spilling over the first of the stone bridges. Pretty soon all the bridges would be impossible to cross and she'd have to walk the distance from the highway to the canyon mouth. But that didn't bother Ruby T. She welcomed the chance to stretch her muscles and feel the power of her body. She could cover the entire distance in forty minutes flat, faster than anyone she knew. And she felt like—what was that guy's name—Paul Bunyan doing it.

Striding over the earth like a giant. Only that bitch, Aires, made her feel weak, like a cream puff in the oven. Disgusted with her thoughts, Ruby T popped the clutch, inching up the last few feet to the bridge at the end of the road. The bridge here was already a foot under water, a clear ice-cold profusion flowing out of the desert mountains like a miracle. It tumbled down over gigantic rocks and crashed full tilt into the series of stone bridges descending to the desert floor.

Creeping along in low gear, Ruby T swung the truck under a big oak and sat looking through the windshield. The oaks were sparkling with new green leaves. The high quartz cliffs scaled the cloudy sky; the desert surged with power and beauty and squeezed Ruby T's heart with desire for life. She took out her pocket comb and pushed her hair away from her face. The curls that fell over her forehead were a concession to femininity and the world. Now that she was alone, she combed her hair to suit herself—straight back. She had a beautiful face but not a face for everyone to see. The high forehead, the strong cheekbones, the small mouth with distinctly defined lips—this was not the face of a man or the face of a woman. It was a face that appeared on statues in antiquity, a face that appeared painful with exposure. Because beauty is the consummately revealed, and Ruby T hid nothing from herself, or anyone else.

She tucked her Levi's into her boots and crossed the bridge. She dipped her hands and pressed the still cold water to her face, her neck, her hair until she shuddered with cold. She wound a scarf around her neck and put on her jacket and, shrugging, took the trail to the falls.

It wasn't far but she felt as if she were alone in the world, her heart and will climbing a trail that had to be climbed.

Ruby T knew how Aires thought: she hadn't made any promises so there were none to keep. But at the same time she had been careful to keep Ruby T on a tether all winter with her mouth and hands an inch away from unbearable lushness, unthinkable satisfaction.

And then two Sundays ago, on the first blistering hot day of summer, she and Aires had gone to Piedra Blanca to swim. The sky was glittering with sun and a suffocating heat smothered the sandstone cliffs and pursued them all the way to the water's edge. They were alone in a little cove ringed with cattails.

Ruby T wore a pair of faded jeans cut off at the thighs and a too-big sleeveless t-shirt that slid off her strong brown shoulder as she moved, revealing the soft curve of her breast. She looked like butterscotch ice cream just starting to melt, all the more tantalizing because she didn't know it, and Aires would never tell her. Ruby T only had thoughts and eyes for Aires, who had been playing with Ruby T's curls while she was driving, running her fingers up and down Ruby T's arm, straying over her breast and dropping down to tease the inside of Ruby T's bare thighs. Somehow the pickup had managed to stay on the road, but Ruby T was submerged in desire. Aires stepped down to the lake in a black bikini. Giving Ruby T a final, very sexy come-on smile, she dropped her bikini top and slipped into the cool deep water.

Going after her, the water did nothing to cool off Ruby T, who was more than ready to put her lips all the places she herself had been touched on the way there. She came close, her mouth reaching for Aires' breast and the nipple that was hovering just above the water line. At the same time, Ruby T's hands had brushed Aires' thighs and her fingers were about to take hold when, much to Ruby T's incomprehension, Aires slid away with a toss of her head. She only went to lay on the sand, but she was gone. Gone to wherever she always went once she had Ruby T panting, as though Ruby T was a complete stranger making strange uninvited suggestions.

Ruby T's utter confusion, not to mention utter frustration, at being pulled so close and then left standing in a lake, sent her into a spinning fall from the edge of the world. She had appeared at Ma Pache's door, pale and shaking, thirsting like a hummingbird.

"Don't be a stupid india," Ma Pache had said. "Deshacete de esa gringa!" Ma Pache saw nothing wrong in using racial epithets whenever she felt like it, especially when it came to protecting her favorite granddaughter. "Don't let that white girl make a fool of you," she had scolded, her cheeks shaking like jello.

They were on the patio. Ma Pache sat in her big wicker chair like a queen, legs planted, hands gesturing as if she were pronouncing judgments. Having outlived her parsimonious husband by twenty years, she profited immensely and joyfully from what had been a lifetime of her own work. Now the ranch whose fields she had worked with child after child on her back was hers, and she had divided it among her family. In return they each gave her a monthly fee, which paid for anything she desired.

Ruby T sat on the steps at Ma Pache's feet, enjoying the shade of the old oak which dominated the courtyard. "Well, you know how it is," she said, trying to justify her painful feelings. "We can't always pick whom we love."

"Ay, mi hita, let me tell you something," said Ma Pache. "You have to make your own happiness yourself and choose others who will do it with you. Otherwise, you'll always be crying. The sooner you understand this, the better."

Ruby T grunted. It would have been disrespectful to contradict Ma Pache, but also, she didn't have an answer.

Why did she love Aires, that round-eyed little snip with breasts like fresh mangos and hips that moved as deliciously as a field of green waving grass in summer heat? "That's what I get for getting my hands wet," she said to herself. "Now I'm sunk. She's twisting me around like a pig's tail, like the thread on a Thai stick, like the wire around a garbage sack. What am I gonna do? What am I gonna do?"

At the falls Ruby T stuck her heated face into the rushing stream and then sat on a boulder, her feet dangling an inch above the breaking, curdling, foaming sled of water. It stormed and bubbled, but there was nothing the water could do. It crashed against the rocks and slid away from them like grease. Maybe some place it came to rest in a mild pool, but here the water was sheer thunder and iced violence. Ruby T's heart drifted on the river's lap with gratitude, her very teeth rattling from the sound of it, her senses deluged in it, her breast filled with incoherent rash desires. She imagined plunging headlong into the water, falling forever with just the beating of her heart and the blood rushing inside of her.

Wet with spray, she climbed away from the water up to a ledge that jutted out from the canyon face like a bucktooth.

The entire winter Aires had pulled Ruby T close and then backpedaled away. Now it was the beginning of summer and, climbing out on the ledge alone, Ruby T knew a lonely hungry woman on top of a mountain was the last straw. It was a personal disaster she could not abide. Here she sat, in triumphant splendor, all by herself. She whistled a few notes and then sang as loudly as she could,

> "Her face is like an angel's,
> but her heart is cold as ice,
> and that's not nice, not nice,
> not nice!"

Each time Ruby T saw Aires, she was hooked and dangled all over again. "Shit," said Ruby T, "she's gonna suck all the blood out of me till I fall down dead. Well, guess what? I'm not gonna let her anymore." Frantic with unspent energy and without the slightest idea what she was going to do, Ruby T rushed back down the trail, slipping and sliding on the steep ground. She drove the truck out of there, bouncing and clattering over loose rocks, the suspension taking the stone bridges like a bucking horse. She drove the rest of the way to the border without stopping until she got to the border crossing at 2 Rock.

"Anda, mujer!" said the border guard. "Parece que te huistes de un demonio."

"Yeah, running from devils—that's exactly how it is sometimes," said Ruby T, looking at her mud-encrusted wheels. She climbed back in and drove across the border down a potholed street and parked the truck alongside an iron fence that looked like someone had taken big bites out of it with dull teeth. She gave two kids "fifty cents now and fifty cents later" to watch the 4x4. They crawled up on the hood, chattering in rapid Spanish, and sat there like kings on a throne, grinning, their dirty faces sweet with innocence and happiness. Ruby T couldn't remember the last time she had felt like that. Maybe it was the first time Aires had touched her face with her fingers and passed that current of electricity into her, stopping Ruby T in her tracks. She had been running full throttle in first gear ever since. Innocence? Happiness? Ruby T's desire was always like that, innocent, fresh, as though this tightening of muscles, this desperate longing of the soul had only just been born. Springing up, defying all constraint, like new skin casting off the old and exposing a new species of life. Maybe this was what made Aires touch Ruby T in the first place, entice her and then hold herself away, hang Ruby T dangling half out of water like a hooked fish. Aires wasn't cruel, just lacking the gift of pleasure. Having none herself, she chose to steal it from others. And stealing from Ruby T was the easiest thing she'd ever done.

Anyway, here was Ruby T walking down the cobblestoned street of Dos Piedras, rickety, like an old brittle rubber band, and suddenly everything got familiar again: the childhood smell of

Mexican cloth from piles of blankets on vendor tables; the shadowy interiors of small stores sparkling with crystal glasses. The faces of the salespeople—eager, smiling—invaded Ruby T's body like warm loving comfort.

She relaxed. Just crossing the invisible line of the border, she found the world was generous again. Promises of warm skin, delicate fingers, burning hearts flooded through her, along with the mouth-watering smells of pan de huevo and tacos and tortillas, leather, and coca and chili colorado, manzanilla, yerba santa and freznil, and chocolate and pure vanilla. Fruit from the interior, piña and mangos and papayas and aguacates were piled high in fruit stalls, surrounded by drunken flies.

Life was in Ruby T, and at this moment she owned the world that was stolen every time she went near Aires and became hollow with desire and love. She yearned for just this kind of freedom, but her heart still shrank as though pierced by a rusty nail at the thought of abandoning her love for Aires—love that flowed in rivers of red; thick, pungent and eager for more—Ay, Amor! Ruby T shut her heart out of the conversation but her face lost its happiness. She was weaving again by the time she reached the Dos Piedras Cafe.

The Cafe sat on the edge of yesterday, barely holding onto the tail of tomorrow: a small squat house of pink and blue stucco. In a dim window, almost hidden by thick and thorny cholla, hung a neon sign, lit day and night. There were two leafy banana trees by the path leading to the door and a plaster donkey with faded paper flowers around his neck. The donkey's feet were encircled by rows of Pepsi and Coca-Cola bottle caps.

"I love this place," said Ruby T when she got inside. Each wall was a different color: green, yellow, white and blue. A veladora was burning as always under an ancient statue of La Guadalupe. And the customers were familiar too: las dos Hermanitas de San Francisco in their brown habits and beaded rope belts, heads bobbing and smiling as they whispered to each other. Old Isidro, hands wrapped around a steaming cafe, his ragged coat buttoned with safety pins, blowing and sipping from his cup. Two of las mujeres de la calle, Veronica and Rosita, always there between hits, were like fixtures in the Dos Pedras Cafe. At the moment they were smoothing their nylons with sensuous fingers, nails painted red and green. In this mishmash of gente, Ruby T was home.

"Orale, Rubia, que haces aqui?" It was Tomasa peering through the window from the kitchen. "What's up?"

"No se," said Ruby T truthfully. Her legs were weak and she sat down at the nearest table.

"Pero mira no mas como vienes," said Tomasa so everyone could hear, "Quien te pico, mujer?"

"I guess someone *did* bite me," said Ruby T wryly, sweat breaking out on her forehead. Las dos mujeres de la calle laughed in a friendly way. Veronica came over and started rubbing Ruby T's shoulders with strong supple fingers and Ruby T melted, leaning back against Veronica's stomach, just beneath the warm curve of her breasts. Her tenderness covered Ruby T like a blanket.

"That's enough," said Rosita, "you're putting her to sleep." Both women laughed, but Ruby T was trembling again. Veronica pulled a handkerchief out of her sleeve and fanned her with it.

"Mira," said Rosita, serious now, "there's only one way to shed a mal amor. You have to lie down with scorpions."

"Are you kidding?" Ruby T squeaked. She felt like she'd already walked a hundred miles just to reach the Dos Piedras Cafe; if she had to do anything else courageous, she'd drop dead.

"No keeding, keed," said Rosita, kidding, but not kidding. Her eyes were like black coals. "If you want to free yourself from a bad love, you have to lie down with scorpions, y con eso, te curas para siempre. That's all it takes," she declared. Rosita was dead serious. Ruby T's heart rose to her throat, but she felt her spirit already squirming around to a position of bravery. She knew there was really no solution to this bleeding passion for Aires except to launch herself beyond it, and only something extreme would make her take that precipitous leap.

"Christ!" she said.

"No—pura de la Madre," said Rosita, and kissed her fingers in the direction of La Guadalupe.

An hour later, fortified with empanada de guava and cafe, Ruby T and Rosita were struggling up Loma Prieta. Ruby T thought she was in shape, but her breath was coming in gasps trying to keep up with Rosita, who was carrying her high heels and climbing like a goat, the muscles in her skinny legs standing out like small coconuts.

"Listen, kid, I'm taking this time out from work for *you*," she said, without losing a breath. She looked back at Ruby T. "Para que no digas que no fui tu hermana, okay? Us women gotta stick together, and that's all."

Ruby T grunted and bumped into Rosita as the trail reached its high point and took a sudden dip onto a little flat area ringed with ocotillo. Inside the enclosure mango and avocado trees grew in profusion, their large leaves shading a small wooden house. Next to it was a small open stable. A donkey was standing there, perfectly still. Rosita carefully closed the high gate after them. The ground on both sides of the path looked like the skin of a clay bowl that had been polished with a stone, hard and smooth and glowing. On one side was a stone relief of Coyolxauhqui, the moon goddess, and on the other side was a stone sculpture of Coatlicue, her mother.

Ruby T saw the house and everything about it all at the same time, and thought, I will not be the same when I come out again. She was seized by a feeling of exhilaration almost indistinguishable from panic—which was actually very much like the blossoming of ecstasy. Her feet stumbled, unsure whether to go forward or turn and run. Rosita clasped her arm with a firm and encouraging grip. There was a second of profound mutual respect, and then both women giggled and moved toward the door.

It was a wonderful summer afternoon. Ruby T was sitting at Ma Pache's feet while the old woman played lovingly with her curls. She had told Ma Pache all about it in bits and pieces in the order in which it all made sense to her. And now she was telling her the end: perennial darkness permeated the house that was like a cave, but she could see everything. There was a fire burning in the hearth where there were only rocks. She had been drinking tea, her legs stretched out in front of her, staring at the flames. How sharply bright the woman's eyes became, like superbly cut diamonds. Her fingernails were easily seven inches long, and her skirt began to move like snakes. The bruja took a sharp knife and opened the breast of a sparrow, placing the still hot and beating heart in Ruby T.'s mouth.

"Jijole!" said Ma Pache. "When you go in a witch's house, never drink anything! You know they always put something in it."

"That's not all," said Ruby T.

The bruja held a mirror in front of Ruby T. "One is you, and one is a ghost that has attached itself to you."

Both faces in the mirror grinned back at Ruby T. "How do I know which one is me?" she asked.

The bruja put one taloned hand on Ruby T.'s shoulder. "One is made of all your incorrect desires, tus mentiras."

"But how can desires be true or false?"

One of the faces answered her, "Lo que no se da no se debe, pero tampoco vale."

"What?" said Ruby T.

"Ssh, ssh," said the bruja. "You are very good at confusing yourself, and while what you say is true, it is also useless. That's how most truths are."

"Humph! I knew that!" said Ma Pache. She tugged Ruby T.'s curls and the younger woman laughed.

"Don't you want to know what happened?"

"Haber, digame."

"She broke the mirror," said Ruby T.

"Quien? La bruja?"

"No. Me. The me in the mirror that thought she knew everything. The other one just kept laughing. I could see her laughing all over the cracked mirror."

"Cabrona!" said Ma Pache.

"No, see, when I realized I couldn't figure anything out with my head, it was a good thing."

"Then who was the one who laughed? The real you?"

"No, listen..."

The bruja waited. Ruby T was entranced by the laughing face in the mirror. Then she grabbed the mirror and was going to throw it in the fire, but the bruja stopped her. She took Ruby T outside and told her to dig a hole, put the cracked mirror in the hole and cover it with dirt.

"Was that all?" asked Ma Pache.

"That was the easy part," said Ruby T. "That was just to see if she wanted to work with me or not. The hard part was when I woke up in a round hole in the ground with nothing but a grass mat over me."

Ruby T had been shivering for a long time, trying not to wake up. She sat up, saw that she was naked, therefore cold, but more than anything she wanted to know what was that scratching sound? Then she saw the scorpions like little wind-up toys, unwinding. They were clavadas to the grass mat by their tails and wriggling. Ruby T leaped out of the hole, flinging the grass mat to the ground. The twelve stuck scorpions came loose and scurried away in the direction of the mango trees. She never saw the scorpion that had been clinging demurely to one of her curls fall to the ground and land in the hole, because she was jumping up and down, screaming. The tiny brown scorpion scrambled out and took off after the others. The donkey flattened his ears and bayed.

The bruja came out of the little house and held up one finger to her lips. With this motion, Ruby T's fear vanished. The reality of the night she had gone through was like leavening—she was filled with herself. The bruja motioned Ruby T inside and handed her her clothes. Ruby T was dressed before she noticed she was looking at a middle-aged woman in a print dress. The dress had little pink and green mangos on it. The woman smiled and asked her if she'd like some cafe con leche, and without waiting for her answer, brought it to her in a small yellow cup with matching saucer. Then she told Ruby T, "En boca cerrada no entran moscas." Ruby T closed her mouth.

The same day Ruby T went to the tattoo parlor across the border on the American side. The tattoo artist looked like a blacksmith but handled the needles with the delicacy of a gem cutter. Ruby T was not surprised.

"Are you sure the needles didn't hurt your heart?" asked Ma Pache, concerned.

"Naw, they were good for it," said Ruby T, showing Ma Pache the tattoo again, just above her heart. It was an exquisitely executed skull with a red rose between its teeth. The letters on its forehead spelled A-M-O-R. Ruby T knew she'd always have a lot to think about every time she saw it. Her memories were still new, but becoming part of her slowly and surely. Especially the one of when she had casually walked into the Matador Bar. Aires had been there with one of her male friends. Ruby T had walked up to her, absorbing the woman she had loved so much with one encompassing glance: the eyes of gorgeous blue fire, the lush, red, cascading hair, the lightly tanned skin. Ruby T had taken her face and, for one brief second, kissed her mouth, and let her go.

The man beside Aires started to get up, but Ruby T had already turned and walked away. He shrugged his shoulders and went back to his gin and tonic. Ruby T didn't see the look on the other woman's face, the way Aires lifted trembling fingers to her lips. Ruby T was outside, jumping into her truck. She took the road to Dos Piedras, filled with gleeful anticipation. She was invited to a barbocoa de chivito by a woman with long black braids and the countenance of a saint who, nevertheless, challenged Ruby T with her eyes and licked her lips with a tongue of fire.

Coming of Age

It was mid-October and strong winds from the northern mountains spun around the desert floor. Pochie had not found any coal on the tracks for a long time. She walked up and down, looking first into the hazy distance ahead, and then back where the telephone poles shrank into toothpicks. There was nothing on the tracks anywhere, except one water tank that made the trains stop. Pochie stood, brown hair in her face, thin, tense, as if waiting for what had already happened to her to reach her, for the heat and smells and tastes, the pain to catch up to her. But she was too far away now. What had happened had settled into the hidden flesh of her body.

Shaking a little, tears drying undiscovered on her face, Pochie saw the railroad tracks, the spreading desert, and the eternally present sky that was filling up with huge, round thunderheads. With stiff fingers she pulled her torn sweater closer around her, ignoring the cramping in her stomach. She decided to keep walking south, toward the Mexican border. Maybe trains coming from there had dropped something worth picking up, something that would burn and make her warm. So she followed her intermittent shadow south.

When Pochie couldn't walk anymore, she sat down on the edge of a rail, staring at the southern mountains. The blood had long ago dried on her fingers, but the pain came in big gulps that bent her in two. In a wave of nausea, she threw up on the few blades of grass that grew between the tracks. Nothing came out but acid bubbles that burned her mouth. It was fitting because her spirit was like a sour pozo where water no longer flowed.

She found a clean piece of grass and stuck it between her teeth and chewed it. It made her forget the throwing up and gave her something to do with her mouth, which felt strange, like the mouth belonging to another.

The place where Pochie sat was already a different place; the desert had changed from familiar to unknown. She no longer knew the mesquites by sight, nor the spaces between them leading to well-worn trails. Where she was now, the ironwood grew in thick gnarled trunks. Their knotted ancient bodies made shelter for gophers and pack rats, who lived in snug little burrows, hollowed-out pockets created by the living roots.

For an instant the sun came out from the billowing clouds, warming her and releasing a covey of sparrows that flew, chirping sweetly, overhead. Pochie remembered she had almost been that happy once. It was when her friend Sophie LaRue, la negra, had gotten her pants on backward. She jumped into them the wrong way because someone had yelled, as a joke, that the boys were peeking around the corner of the lockers in P.E. They had laughed so hard, Pochie almost peed. Pochie thought that laughter, which had sent delicious waves through her body, must be happiness.

But that seemed like a long time ago, before she was sixteen and her stepfather, Rocha, made her quit school to take care of the house. He had to work, he said, why shouldn't she? Besides, she was too dumb to learn anything, just like her mother Ester had been. But Pochie knew something was wrong, because her mother hadn't been dumb. Ester was smart enough to teach herself how to read English from the newspaper. At night, when Rocha was snoring and stinking of cheap tequila, Pochie remembered falling asleep in her lap, listening to mamita sounding out the strange words one by one, whispering in Pochie's ear, "Ya ves, m'hija, aprende tu tambien para que puedas hacer algo con tu vida. Learn, Pochie, so you can be somebody in life." And Pochie remembered staring at Mama through half-closed lids, falling asleep with her eyes open.

But this memory was spoiled by the memory of Rocha lying there in his sweat-stained pants, the waist folded over under his greasy belly with the black hairs coming out of the navel. And then, one time, his thing hanging out of his pants, and he was watching her face when she saw it, over her mama's shoulder. After that, every time he lay down, there by the stove, he would grunt and show her his thing, even though she didn't want to see it. One time, just one time, Ester saw him, and then he pretended, Ayi Dios, what a big surprise, making a show of turning his back to arrange himself, and Pochie just went outside until she could stop shaking. She was big then, and knew what it was, knew she had to avoid getting near it, no matter what. And then for a few weeks after Ester died, he sat by the cold stove, not eating, drinking, and begging Pochie to come over so he could cry on her pecho, but she didn't. He started making her stay home from school. "Your mama would have wanted you to take care of me," he said. And then the worst thing of all, he started watching her, watching her every move, and finally—this morning. She started to retch with the memory, down on her knees, trying to basquear the taste from her mouth.

When she could, Pochie got up and walked a few feet into the desert. She found some yerba buena growing out of the ribs of a dead saguaro, and she rubbed it on her teeth and between her hands, covering her face with it, breathing in the rich green smell like rain water on desert earth.

When Nuncio was a small boy he loved the desert so much he would curl up in the dirt under a mesquite and lie there for hours. He watched the ants scurrying around, carrying scraps into their hole, which had dirt piled up at the entrance like a little mountain. He rested his head on his arms until he was eye level to the ants and could see everything: all kinds and colors of seeds, bits of plants, and the carcasses of insects. Caterpillar parts and fly's wings seemed to be favorites.

When it was hot, Nuncio found coolness in the breezes under a mesquite. When it rained, he sheltered there too, knees against his chest, arms wrapped around his legs. He gazed out at the lomitas dusted with rain drops, alive and moving under cloud shadows. The sparse branches of the mesquite were just enough to keep him from getting really wet. But in those moments he was enough like the hills, enough like the sage bushes and cactus, that the rain only dusted him too. His hair and skin shone, as though covered with a thin coat of oil. In those moments of perfection, he saw no reason to move, or walk, or eat. He hardly even breathed.

In those childhood days only meanings that passed among cactus and mountains spoke to Nuncio. The distance between the top of a saguaro and the mountain peak behind it told him something. He saw the mountain grow more intensely violet, more vibrant than the yellow green of the cactus, and their relationship was revealed suddenly, starkly, bursting in his consciousness. That was what moved him. Lifting himself from the earth that had nested around him, seeing how the mesquite placed him in space, he knew other things too. He saw creatures, the morning dove, the grey mockingbird, the bobcat and javalina, the lizards, horned toads, tarantulas and scorpions, all like himself, existing unattached to the earth but contained in her embrace. And that was the only world he knew.

Where Nuncio lived, at the south end of the small Mexican border town, pigs ran wild, splashing in the muddy gutters, occasionally chased and beaten by small children with big sticks. In a vast field on the other side of the road, tall wooden barrancas painted red surrounded the bullring. Like the shell of an egg, the barrancas protected the soft center of the ring: the flat yellow sand, cleaned and tended and swept every day, lying smooth and unbroken until Sunday...when strangely, unexpectedly, shrieks of a gored horse burst the air, and streaks of heavy dark blood flung down lines against the pale yellow of the sandy ring, breaking it open.

It was on such a Sunday afternoon, standing in the hot glare of the sun, that Nuncio suddenly awoke—or so it seemed to him. He was eighteen years old and it was the day of his initiation as a matador, the first time he alone had brought the bull all the way to this, the moment of truth. He felt the tall slender strength of his young man's body, his left wrist holding the muleta, loose and sensitive to the slightest deviation in the air. In his right hand he held the estoque, sighting along the length of it, motionless as the bull who waited a few feet away.

The bull's blood still leaked in rivulets from the cluster of banderas nailed to the back of his neck. The strong neck muscles, weakened by pain and exhaustion, allowed the head to fall low, and the bull's breath scattered tiny grains of sand as he gasped for air.

Nuncio felt the fear leave his body with a rush, pushing back the crazed thundering mass of people, who only a moment before had been screaming their heads off. Silence closed in upon the center of the ring. When the moment became absolute, the way it had been in the desert of his childhood when he was like sage under raindrops, Nuncio fanned the muleta a fraction of an inch away from his body, signaling the bull. The bull seemed to glide toward him as Nuncio went up on his toes, the weight of his body moving forward to meet the bull. Guiding the horns past his body with the muleta, he stiffened his fingers and slid the estoque into the bull's spine.

The sound crashed over him again and he almost fell, seeing what he had accomplished: the bull's legs crumbling as though they had been kicked out from under him, his head extended, his tongue hanging useless, blood melting into the sand. At the last moment before he turned away, Nuncio saw the pride, the fierce beautiful strength, the firm flesh of the animal, turn to water. Death drank the bull's life until nothing was left but a loose and shapeless mass. The bull was dragged away by a team of mules as Nuncio, holding up the bull's ears, circled the ring to the blaring of trumpets while the crowd praised him, the new matador.

Later, "Ahi que hombre, que macho eres ahora," the older men said, pressing on him cojones con salsa picada fried in butter. It was his due, they said, and would increase his manhood even more. The smile plastered on his face, he smeared the mess around on his plate, pretending to eat and swallow. The others were too excited to notice the tenderness, the sensitivity in his fingers holding the fork, picking up the shot glass. In those hours while Nuncio was drinking tequila and the others were celebrating, the brave bull's meat was cooking in the hovels past San Cristobal Street, where the dirt path became nameless, descending down into the misery of "El Hoyo." The bull had been apportioned and given to the poor who gathered every Sunday at the rear gate, sweating, anxious to hear the roar of a kill that meant food in their stomachs.

What Nuncio was thinking about while he tipped his glass was the sound of the bull's breathing. It was like a bellows, the huge chest and ribcage rising and falling, blowing out the air, fanning it into a flame that came out his eyes and reached into the razor-sharp tips of his horns. That sound—of life—had been ended by him, Nuncio. That life and death existed side by side, he thought, was terrible.

Nuncio's primo, who was also his segundo, had taken him home afterward and lowered him tenderly onto the bed, turning his head so he could vomit over the side if he needed to and leaving him alone to sleep. But he had not slept; he had drowned in the bull's breath, swathed and purified by the bull's rough skin, cradled in the bull's sweat, and kissed by his horns. So Nuncio awakened and cried beneath the hot gush of water, standing in the shower stall in his clothes until he could bear to rip them from his body. He tore them into rags. He didn't want anything from that day. He didn't want his own life. He needed to be forgiven, but death neither condemns nor forgives. Death is nothing.

That morning Nuncio followed the railroad tracks out into the desert. At last he could no longer hear his thoughts; he couldn't remember or feel what it had been like to kill the bull, the shock to his own soul. Nuncio and the desert were alone.

"Ahora si, que eres mujer," Rocha had told her. "A girl does not become a woman until she bleeds for a man." He fixed his pants as Pochie lay there, blood running down her legs.

"Get out of here and clean yourself," he'd said with disgust, and Pochie went. She kept on going, not thinking, not planning anything, until here she was, sitting by a dead saguaro in the middle of the desert.

It had not rained. The clouds had risen as far as possible into the sky, mushroomed and glowered grey and held. Now the mountain looked different, softer, paloverde branches smears of yellow green brush strokes everywhere on the slopes like the skirts of dancing girls at a baile. Then suddenly the clouds squeezed together. Thunder crashed and echoed, lightning sizzled on the hillsides and rain reached down in a torrent, without curve, without delicacy, just definite flowing strength of sky falling to earth. Pochie held her nose as she sprawled on her back on the ground and opened her mouth. She gulped and spit, chewed yerba buena leaves and spit everything out. She took off her dress and stood naked to the rain, shivering, her hands cupped over her breasts. As if by agreement, the water yielded to a rush of wind and left her, moving north, dark fan to the ground. The sun appeared and Pochie was immediately warmed by its glow. She wrung out her dress and put it on, and, with her sweater for a pillow, she sighed and closed her eyes. She was asleep in a moment, her breast faintly rising and falling like a child's.

When it first started raining, Nuncio ran for an ironwood tree. Then, thirsty and grateful, he too gave himself to the rain. The liquor that had bled from him in sweat and dried on his skin ran from his body in streams. When the rain passed and the wind swept his face he opened his eyes and saw Pochie asleep on the ground. His body shook as if he had been struck.

His stumbling on the rocks woke Pochie with a start, and she yelled the first words in her mind, "What are you looking at?"

Nuncio, frozen where he stood, said, "I thought you were dead."

And Pochie cried, "I want to be dead! I want to be dead!"

Nuncio walked over to her carefully and sat down near to her.

"Me too," he said quietly, and was lost again at once in his own mind. He forgot what he had apprehended only a moment ago—the crushed and defeated body of a woman lying against the earth—the same woman who was still able to turn to him now and ask him, "Why?"

"Because yesterday I killed something important to me, algo sagrada como mi vida," he said. And he told her about the kid he'd been, smart and quick, doing anything he could to get near the matadores, until they started training him. They loved his courage, oh, how they loved him; all of them drunk on death.

As Nuncio spoke, he remembered what he had been in the beginning. He remembered a small boy who could put out his hand and remain kind enough for a wild rabbit to nose his fingers. It was with a shock that he heard Pochie say, bitterly, "There are only one kind of men in the world."

Nuncio shook his head, pleading, "Not me!" But Pochie stood up slowly and walked away from him without looking back.

"I didn't want to be like that!" Nuncio shouted frantically. And suddenly his life eclipsed in his mind: the dying eyes of the bull, the sweet trembling of a rabbit in that long ago childhood...Pochie's wild and suffering eyes.

"I'm sorry!" he cried after her, but she didn't turn around.

Pochie walked south, not thinking about forgiveness, toward the Loma Prieta mountains. Nestled in its flanks was the little town of Jacinto, and a destiny she would never have been able to imagine, waiting for her.

The Painter
and the Vampire

Maybe you'll say I couldn't have known all I'm going to tell you. Maybe you'll say I made it up, but hey, why should I do that? As my ma used to say, I see what I see y no solamente con ojos. And I know me.

It was an awesome, spectacular, extraordinary, pinche night. Ferocious glowering clouds had massed up over the mountains all afternoon and when night gathered it was like a glove smothering the light. Jagged gashes of dry lightning ripped the darkness—bolts of angry crisp fire striking home with a hissing like snakes. And putting a mean susto into everybody. Las casitas along Telesfora Street, hecho de adobe with their brave wooden doors and innocent screened faces, were sullen and sour, like chaperones at a quinceniera party. The thunder that burst over the Barrio could have been mountains crashing to the ground. The earth shook. While out at the bar where we were, here at Four Corners, the tumbleweeds were blowing against the walls and lining up like cranky mustangs with burrs under their tails.

It was the kind of weather I know had Misha walking around the studio like a caged leopard. She wouldn't be able to paint because she'd be right there with the storm, eating it—but starving—beyond words, beyond paint, glowing with raw information, transformed into fluid time. I can just see it: the sounds of Misha's own steps bring her back to the room and to Hail Mary snuffling at the door and looking at her with big expressive German shepherd eyes. She is no ordinary dog. Let's get out in it, her eyes say, and besides, you have an appointment to keep at Four Corners.

"What kind of an appointment?" asks Misha, a little miffed at Hail Mary's presumptuousness. Hail Mary's expression speaks louder than words: it is an if-I-told-you-you-wouldn't-go kind of look.

Outside Misha can't hear herself calling the dog above the howling wind. She is pushed back one step for every two she takes to the driveway and is slammed against the jeep while trying to open the door. Hail Mary, ears laid back, scampers back and forth with her tail whipping and finally climbs in. Misha struggles to close the doors and starts the engine. They roar off in our direction.

When the desert blows you can expect everything—rocks, bushes, telephone poles—to come crashing into your face at any second. The jeep skids from one side of the road to the other like a scrap of paper. Dust blows in all directions, making visibility almost zero. Every time the jeep hits the shoulder, Misha says "Shit!" and Hail Mary digs her snout into her paws a little deeper. When Misha is scared she says shit a lot.

Teeth clenched and knuckles white, Misha drove up to Four Corners just as the sky cracked open with a massive burst of thunder. The rain came down suddenly and hard. Hail Mary whined and yapped at the large drops of water bouncing and steaming off the hood. When Misha got out, Hail Mary let her breath out with a groan and settled down to wait.

Little Lulu and I, Carolina's my name, were setting up the cocktail glasses behind the bar when our longtime customer and friend busted through the doors like duendes were after her.

"Well, look who's here," said Little Lulu. The name was an affectionate gift from her friends, because my business partner was a big woman and her voice fit her size. "Honey, I don't smell any of your usual turpentine perfume. What happened, no visions today?"

"I was...too much going on," said Misha. She looked at me—lusty curly-headed knifeblade of a chicana, that's me, and I got right to the point. I fixed Misha with a telling smile and licked my lips.

"All right—what?" Misha was afraid to ask.

"Aw, give her a chance to get her throat wet," said Little Lulu generously. She already had Misha's favorite in front of her. Misha lifted the bottle and let the ice-cold Tecate gurgle down her throat before she even sat down. There was salt and ice on the lip just the way she liked it, and I bet it bit deliciously.

"There's someone you have to—will—meet," I said, filling my voice with sensuous anticipation, the kind Misha couldn't resist.

She gulped her beer. I could see a familiar tingle going up her spine. "No way, I'm still getting over the last one."

That was just the kind of challenge I like. "Andale, mujer!" I told her. "This is a night made for love. Think of it: her eyes piercing you like lightning, your hearts beating like thunder, kisses furious like the wind!" I topped off the pyramid of glasses I was wiping. "Besides, it'll give you something to paint," I said intentionally.

"That's not why, or what, I paint," said Misha, more than a little touchy. "On the contrary, it interferes with my work." She pronounced the word "work" as though it were in a foreign language. "It interferes with my whole life!" The word "life" was in that foreign language too.

Finally Little Lulu jumped in. "I know you're just aching for some soft exposure," she suggested, her large calloused hands handling the margarita glasses like they were thimbles. I could see the tingle run up Misha's spine again.

"Aching or not," she said.

That was the only way Misha could talk about making love with a woman—like she was a picture hanging way over there on a wall. Not me! I started to say, "Don't you get absolutely loca in that studio all day? Don't you just..." but Misha knew what I was going to say next, and I guess she wasn't in the mood for any of this woman's pronouncements on singles and sex.

"Forget it," she said definitively. "I'm just here to drink my beer."

"Sure you are," said Little Lulu. She patted Misha's hand and nodded me over to the other end of the bar. We went on setting up but we couldn't avoid throwing a few indirectas, suggestive glances at Misha now and then.

Misha straddled her bar stool, trying to calm down from the frustrating inactive day and the harrowing drive to Four Corners. I know what it's like to go out in a storm: the mountains disappear in the darkness so you can't tell where you are and the wind feels like it's pushing you off the edge of the world into nothing. But in the bar we kept the lights low and tasteful—my idea—and Misha's eyes drew in the light reflecting from the mirrors around her. It was the same kind of rose and golden light that flows from flesh in the heat of love. Misha made the connection with her painter's eye; she gave visual phenomena her entire attention, eyes bright with passion. Too bad for everybody that the passion never got as far as her alma too, but maybe that's my personal prejudice. But this isn't about me. So anyway, the story: the kind of passion of the soul I mean is why Angelique appeared in this tiny place, in a vast wild desert on a black and storming night.

Months would go by and then Angelique would come out of nowhere and go away again. So it is easy to imagine how it would have been had they never met...how Misha would have finished a Tecate or two, played a few tunes on the box, and taken herself and a bored Hail Mary home...how her days and months of painting and isolation, with an occasional fling largely forgotten by the next night, would have continued regularly and predictably. But I think Guadalupe must have been watching, because by the time Misha put down her first empty bottle and before she ordered another, it was already too late for it not to happen.

Era su destino, not too soon and not too late. Because Angelique had come and she was waiting in the farthest corner of the bar. She claimed the darkness as her own and her glance had already pierced the impersonal armor Misha wore. Como una rosa on a hot summer's night is how open Angelique was. Misha didn't know anything had happened to her, of course. She was seeing only her own face in the mirror.

Angelique, on the other hand, knew exactly what she was made of and what was inescapable to her living. How did I know that? I see a lot of things from behind the bar and maybe I saw something no one else saw. It was the night of the roller derby when the chicana team came down from Phoenix and was celebrating in the bar afterward. When Angelique wanted that woman skater, she didn't hide it. It wasn't that she said or did anything. She had too much taste for that. But she didn't have to; desire poured out of her with the kind of light I've only seen in church—like the saints worshipping God—that kind of ecstasy, you know?

That's how Angelique looked at that woman, with all of her body. The whole team was drinking Bud and shouting up a storm the way it is after a roller derby. But I could see the shock run through the woman from across the room when she realized Angelique had...chosen her. It was six steps over to Angelique's table and the woman walked them like she was covering the distance between the earth and the moon, one step at a time.

What Angelique's red hair would look like spread out on a black silk sheet was something to think about. Anyway, it didn't matter to Angelique that skaters hate outsiders coming on to one of their own, and a couple of the tough chukas were fingering their switchblades. All Angelique did was wait and worship. See, even when it was for only one night, she followed the lure of love, sign by sign, paying homage to each sweet impression for the painful yearning desire it brought forth in her heart, in her eyes, in her soul, the exquisite thirst of it. Ay, mujer!

That's how she was, and this time the signs, the feelings, all led here—to this moment when Misha turned in her chair, for no apparent reason, and was caught by Angelique's presence, barely visible in her corner but for the energy that surrounded her. A glow that Misha the painter could see because it was like her own. So she fell in love. In that second when her eyes met Angelique's shining eyes—well, I could see the sparks from where I stood—calló like a ton of bricks.

Misha turned back around, picked up her bottle and put it to her lips. Nothing came out. Then she remembered the bottle was empty. Shit, she said to herself, shit, shit, shit. Through her pounding heart, she asked for a second beer, searching for ground like an artist changing palettes halfway through a painting.

The mirror was no longer red and gold; it was a hundred shades of lavender fractured by a pure emerald green where Angelique sat. The light around Angelique folded in on itself with the sheen of black silk or moonlit water. Misha knew with some part of herself that this woman would not come to her; but if she ventured across the distance between them, she would find that she was expected and awaited. Or she would have known this if she had been capable of coming that far out of herself.

Y la otra? Did Angelique really know what she was letting herself in for? Probably not. But like I said, she never bothered with consequences. Prudence had never been an issue and wouldn't be this time either. Her blood made decisions. Her blood spoke for itself, sangre calling to sangre, and personalities and events fell by the wayside.

So now they were ready. And the night was more than suitable. Misha was wrecked out of her skin by the storm and Angelique was a lightning rod, gathering it all in.

Just then a pickup drove up, the motor raced and the door slammed. A native woman everybody called Blue, from the nearby rez, pushed through the doors, bringing with her wild energy and smells of sweet cactus syrup and outdoor fires. The night rushed in with her, not just rain but a windful of fury, a tempest. A big chiflon shook the walls and blew our hair back, reminding us how vulnerable we really were, and then the doors closed again.

Blue was a familiar face and an artist too. She limped to the bar, asked for a draft, and I drew one for her. She said a few words to Misha. It must have been a bad painting day for her also, because she worked from the source, out in the desert. She once told me it was like "seeing" a thousand voices and distilling them down to a few on canvas. We had one of her paintings on the wall: a grove of mesquites at dusk washed with orange light; you had to look twice to see the coyote peering out of the twisted trunks and tangled branches. Blue never painted people and she didn't speak much either. Her silence was always agreeable.

For a while everybody was saying hello, and then Blue went over to the jukebox. With the storm outside, the small group and the feeling of refuge inside, it didn't feel like a raucous night. Blue punched in some mellow country music and came back to the bar. A few minutes later, Angelique walked over. Everybody stopped what they were doing, especially Misha. And me—I always stared, and I wondered.

It wasn't the way she appeared so much; it was the way she made me feel. I just wanted to look. She made me feel, en el corazon, something that was both pain and delight. I was intensely aware of this particular moment, and I wished the best of human feelings, the love and desire, were being saved up somewhere for la Diosa to give back to us on a rainy day.

I could imagine how an artist must feel, wanting to capture and save that special recognition of life sharpened to a point, el filo de la vida. I could tell the others felt it too. Maybe it was Angelique's eyes: once I saw them I wanted to look at them forever, just to make sure. They were a shade of blue so light they seemed to disappear in air, the large pupils a vibrating luminous black. It wasn't physical attraction she inspired; it was my alma turning inside out because what I knew was so beautiful; all my intentions, good and bad, present and future, were vindicated.

Little Lulu found her voice first. "It's a lousy night and it looks like it's just us, honey, so sit a spell." She had refined to an art the bartender's code of putting people at ease, and she meant every word. Then Misha had to say something too, because it was a matter of personal honor.

"Yes, tell us what exigencies of the spirit brought you here tonight," she said. I almost blurted, "Que?" But Little Lulu threw me a warning glance, the kind that said, Stop watching, but how could I do that? I don't think Misha knew what she was saying herself, but with those words the invisible line between the two women was crossed.

Well, Misha couldn't stand Angelique's eyes on her for more than a second, so she answered her own question. "The music, right?"

"Yes," said Angelique, "yes, move me." Of course I knew what she meant immediately, but Misha swung around and almost fell off her bar stool.

"Dance, I mean. I'm sorry, my English gets in the way. Dance with me."

Misha was shaking like a leaf. She made a point of not looking at me or Little Lulu. I realized we were both staring, so we made ourselves very busy with something under the counter. But by the time the two women were on the dance floor in front of the jukebox, the rest of us didn't exist.

Angelique came close and Misha backed away. Angelique's dress fell in swirls of cobalt blue as she moved, and she said something in a teasing voice. All of a sudden there was something I just had to hear on the jukebox, so I grabbed a handful of quarters from the register and went over there. I know what you're thinking, but like my Ma always said, if you want to know something, go to the source.

Well, they were facing each other. Misha had a painful look on her face like she had just split wide open and didn't feel that great about what had come out. Like getting black paint mixed up with the bright colors.

Misha was saying, "You don't know who I am."

And Angelique said, "I know you better than you think, my dear Misha."

Misha was scared, but they were holding each other by now, with a touch so light it might not have existed, except that the thuds of their hearts were audible to both, drumming across the fast-closing gap between them.

"I am not afraid of anything," Angelique said.

"Fear is healthy; fear is how we survive," Misha insisted, holding back. It was Angelique's decision then, and she made it. This was her reason for being here and there was nothing to wait for. Their bodies came together like liquid dynamite.

I don't think I was watching what my fingers were doing, because the jukebox suddenly came beaming out with the only New Age stuff we had in there. Over and over again, variations of *No matter where you go I will find you*...Blue was moving by herself to the native drum rhythms, in the shadows. Where was the frontier? Where was home? Where were the stars spinning in their universe of motion? This was how Misha and Angelique danced. This was how they were. You can take my word for it.

Then I saw Little Lulu making wild signs at me to get out of there, and I was just going to move when the lights went out. The electricity, that is. In the silence the sounds of the desert storm seemed to break right through the walls, scary, jijole! as if we were all under some terrible death sentence, only to be reprieved the next moment; as if nothing fake could exist any longer, only what was true, and we were all equally vulnerable and responsible.

I found my wits and struck a match, immediately reflected in the mirrors and all the glass. Little Lulu found the emergency candles and we placed them around the bar. Misha and Angelique were still standing there, barely moving, looking at each other.

"Hey, you two," Blue called softly, "the music's over." They came up to the bar, Misha, her face on fire; Angelique, pale as a swan. That something had happened to which they were irrevocably committed was obvious. The candles were burning all around the room now, flickering in the drafts that came out of nowhere. We were floating on charged energy from outside and inside. Blue started picking up her change.

"Maybe you better not try to drive home yet," Little Lulu volunteered. Big kindhearted woman that she was, she was worried, and maybe innocent of where the danger was coming from. But I'll tell you one thing: there were ants crawling up the back of my neck. Blue looked at me, her eyes suddenly gone deep; we both knew something was up. Scratching, scratching, came sounds behind the walls.

"It's just the tumbleweeds moving around in the wind," I said to Little Lulu. Blue took out a sprig of sage—she was never without it. She lit it and limped around the room, letting smoke from the burning end curl up toward all the dark corners. When the door was flung open, everybody jumped.

"What's the matter with you ladies? You look like you seen a ghost." It was only Pepe from the Double R. "Cabrones, it's hell outside. Give me a shot," he said, flipping a silver dollar on the bar.

"Vienes solo? No one else?" I asked him.

"Naw, Bolsas is right behind me," he said, and I'm thinking, Christ, old Bolsas! He was called that—"Bags"—because he had a habit of picking up everything in sight and taking it home in his pockets. Shot glasses, toothpicks, napkins, ashtrays, olives, cherries, chips, paper towels and rolls of tissue from the restrooms. One time he even managed to take the doorknob from the toilet door. Other than that, he was an all-right old man. Bueno, better him than something else, I said to myself. Little Lulu was looking at me strangely. Bolsas came in and sat at a table without taking his coat off or saying a word.

"What's the matter with him?" asked Little Lulu.

"Donno, he's been weird like that all evening," said Pepe in a low voice.

"That's all we need," I said.

"So, kick him out," said Pepe, shrugging his shoulders and picking up his whiskey.

"You're a great friend. He's not hurting anything, so as long as it stays that way, he's welcome too," said Little Lulu.

"He's the one that wanted to come," said Pepe. "Walked all the way from the rez to the ranch and wouldn't take no for an answer. And now look at him." Blue went over to Bolsas and said something to him in their language. The old man mumbled something.

"He doesn't want anything to drink," Blue said. "Says he has to stay strong."

"What does he mean?" said Misha. Angelique was at the other end of the bar and glowing like a candle. Then the scratching on the walls came again, only this time it was more like stiff claws raking the ceiling.

"Don't tell me that's tumbleweeds," said Little Lulu, her eyes big. Angelique walked to the door and, before we could say anything, opened it. The wind whipped her dress around her legs. Drops of rain spun in and clung to her red hair, where they shone like diamonds.

The man who entered was beautiful, beautiful like the edge of a cliff, beautiful like a needle dripping heroin in a dark alley, like a honed blade held pressed to a bare throat. He and Angelique could have been brother and sister, the way he looked. He smirked at everybody in the room, especially at Blue, who stood nearby, the little sprig of sage still smoking in her hand. His face lost its smirk when his eyes rested on Angelique. It was replaced by a look of complicit hunger.

"Mira, you," I said. Well, I believe in meeting fire with fire. "Nobody asked you here and nobody wants you here...bloodsucker," I added. The large red ruby at his throat gleamed and he tossed his head, red curls falling to his shoulders.

"She knows how it feels, don't you?" he said to Angelique, his voice like bass notes. His attention turned back to the others and fastened on Misha. "Just thought I'd come and see for myself. You are so long in coming home," he said to Angelique.

"There's nothing to see and there's nothing to drink, either," I said. But he was looking at Misha, licking the red flush on her face with his eyes.

Angelique spoke slowly and distinctly. "C'est à moi, Gerard. Pas de mal, Gerard. Je t'en prie." Her eyes burned a warning.

"Is everybody here nuts or what?" Misha's voice was strident with the beginnings of fear.

"Gerard," I said, "you better leave."

"Whatever the woman wants," said Little Lulu cheerfully, and started coming around the bar toward Gerard. That's when he launched himself toward the ceiling and, in one powerful swoop, descended on Misha, who was rooted to the ground like a stick. She had no choice—Angelique was there first, facing him, her radical teeth bared like razors. Gerard danced through the air in another direction and landed on Little Lulu. As big as she was he was stronger, and in one instant had her at the door. Pepe was stuck to his chair like a block of ice, but Bolsas stood up and pulled an arrow out of his pocket. Without a wasted motion, he leaped. Gerard was fast but the arrow pinned his shirt to the wall, just missing his heart. Little Lulu pulled loose and I rushed at him with a barrio special, a baseball bat with spikes on the end of it. Gerard screamed with rage and jumped on the defenseless Pepe, who could only squeak at the sight of Gerard's looming teeth. But Blue surprised us all. She was already there. She tossed a burning candle and all the sizzling wax that had collected in its tin, into Gerard's face. His screech made our hair stand up, as he blasted through the doors without bothering to open them. What was left of the doors hung from the hinges in tatters, flapping back and forth. The wind blew the candles out, except for the ones on the jukebox which didn't even flicker.

The light was on their faces when Misha said to Angelique, "I have to talk to you." She started shouting, "You were going to suck my blood!"

"No, chérie, I only came to taste your soul," Angelique said in a voice I could barely hear.

Misha was going to say something more when she split open again and, looking inside, saw a hundred paintings on the wall, red and spilling over. She said, "You were stealing me from myself." Cold and distant.

Angelique's eyes were large, her voice low. The rest of us could have been ghosts, Angelique was so focused on Misha, her voice low and intense. "No, you are wrong. Didn't you know it when we touched? Didn't your spirit sing while our bodies burned?"

Misha lied again. "I would have given you anything."

But Angelique knew, and answered, "The ones like you drink all that we are, all that you, yourselves, do not dare to be. You live from our souls until you are sated. And then you imagine yourselves free, without need. You cannot feed me, except by accident, because you are able to give nothing." Her eyes in their tears struck fire and she pressed a hand to her breast. "It is my blood in the heart of your canvas!"

She turned to leave, but looked back at Misha, saying, "Tu n'as rien entendu, ma chère?" which anyone who's had a year of French knows means, "You just don't get it, do you?" But maybe Misha did get something, because when Angelique was gone the sounds breaking from Misha were like brittle glass. Outside in the jeep, Hail Mary howled and howled.

So, asi fue. I, Carolina, was there. All I know is, Angelique's words fell into my blood. I can't take them out, y me muero de sed. If she comes back, I'll be waiting for her. Expecting her. I know she'll feel it too, because now my thirst is like hers. And she can drink from my soul anytime. Ay, mujer!

*K*LEYA FORTÉ-ESCAMILLA was born in a border town and grew up in Baja and southwestern Arizona; with ancestry from Western Europe, Peru and Mexico.

She has two BAs, one in Art, and the other in French/Philosophy, and an MA in Creative Writing. She has published two novels, *Daughter of The Mountain*, and *Mada*, as well as various short stories in journals and anthologies.

Kleya received an Astraea Foundation Award for writing in 1993.

aunt lute books is a multicultural women's press that has been committed to publishing high quality, culturally d   literature since 1982. In 1990, the Aunt Lute Foundation was formed as a non profit corporation to publish and distribute books that reflect the complex truths of women's lives and the possibilities for personal and social change. We seek work that explores the specificities of the very different histories from which we come, and that examines the intersections between the borders we all inhabit.

Please write or phone for a free catalogue of our other books or if you wish to be on our mailing list for future titles. You may buy books directly from us by phoning in a credit card order or mailing a check with the catalogue order form.

Aunt Lute Books
P.O. Box 410687
San Francisco, CA 94141
(415) 826-1300

This book would not have been possible without the kind contributions of the **Aunt Lute Founding Friends:**

Anonymous Donor	Diane Goldstein
Anonymous Donor	Diane Mosbacher, M.D., Ph.D.
Rusty Barcelo	Elise Rymer Turner
Diana Harris	William Preston, Jr.
Phoebe Robins Hunter	